LUMBERJANES

GHOST CABIN

BOOK FOUR

BY MARIKO TAMAKI
ILLUSTRATED BY BROOKLYN ALLEN

BASED ON THE LUMBERJANES COMICS

CREATED BY SHANNON WATTERS,
GRACE ELLIS, NOELLE STEVENSON & BROOKLYN ALLEN

AMULET BOOKS
NEW YORK

CATALOGING-IN-PUBLICATION DATA HAS BEEN APPLIED FOR
AND MAY BE OBTAINED FROM THE LIBRARY OF CONGRESS.
ISBN 978-1-4197-3361-1

PUBLISHED IN 2019 BY AMULET BOOKS, AN IMPRINT OF ABRAMS.

PRINTED AND BOUND IN USA
10 9 8 7 6 5 4 3 2 1

AMULET BOOKS ARE AVAILABLE AT SPECIAL DISCOUNTS WHEN PURCHASED
IN QUANTITY FOR PREMIUMS AND PROMOTIONS AS WELL AS FUNDRAISING
OR EDUCATIONAL USE. SPECIAL EDITIONS CAN ALSO BE CREATED
TO SPECIFICATION. FOR DETAILS, CONTACT
SPECIALSALES@ABRAMSBOOKS.COM OR THE ADDRESS BELOW.

AMULET BOOKS˙ IS A REGISTERED TRADEMARK OF HARRY N. ABRAMS, INC.

ABRAMS The Art of Books
195 Broadway, New York, NY 10007
abramsbooks.com

FOR
NANA,
BEVERLY,
AND
YUKI
—M.T.

LUMBERJANES

FIELD MANUAL

LUMBERJANES PLEDGE

I solemnly swear to do my best

Every day, and in all that I do,
To be brave and strong,

To be truthful and compassionate,
To be interesting and interested,

To pay attention and question
The world around me,

To think of others first,
To always help and protect my friends

~~To~~ ~~~~ *(struck through)* THEN THERE'S A LINE ABOUT GOD, OR WHATEVER

And to make the world a better place

For Lumberjane scouts
And for everyone else.

PART ONE

SOCK IT TO ME!

HIT ME WITH YOUR BEST SOCK

Whether hiking across a mountain trail or through the wild woods, warm dry feet are an essential component to scout well-being.

With this badge, scouts will learn the basics of purl and knit, the component parts that assemble one of the coziest features of the scout uniform.

Sock options include: knee socks, ankle socks, thigh-high socks, wool socks, blended socks, striped socks, toe socks, footie socks, socks with animal prints, polka dots, little pink horses, and little blue alligators.

This badge does not require but encourages scouts to knit pattern socks with tiny dragons hop-scotching with laughing monkeys.

Whether knit or woven, on one needle or two, the most essential part of sock knowledge for this badge is the under-standing of the role socks play in . . .

CHAPTER 1

Not every day at Miss Qiunzella Thiskwin Penniquiqul Thistle Crumpet's Camp for Hardcore Lady-Types is amazing.

MOST of them are.

But some of them are less like sunshine and roses and more like a moose burp in a confined, hot moose stall. Times a hundred.

Some of them are less like fresh bagels and more like the stale cookie you find in the bottom of your knapsack when you're really hungry . . .

Crumby.

This particular day at Miss Qiunzella Thiskwin Penniquiqul Thistle Crumpet's Camp started out deceptively well.

It did rain in the morning, but not hard, more of a light mist, like what comes out of a fancy sprinkler system for a fancy lawn, a mist that made the world outside Molly's window look like a rainbow, and she reached down and booped Mal on the nose so she could see it.

"Look," Molly whispered, pointing.

"Holy Jacqueline Woodson!" Mal gasped, sitting up in bed. "Rainbow connection!"

"RAINBOW!" Ripley cheered, bouncing out of the cabin in order to perform her rainbow celebration dance.

"RIPLEY! SHOES!" April called out, chasing after Ripley with sneakers in hand.

For reasons she couldn't explain, Mal couldn't get rid of the ABBA song that had been playing in her head off and on all summer.

ABBA was in no way Mal's favorite band. But some of their songs are just really happy cheesy songs. And Molly made Mal think of happy cheesy things a lot of the time.

Like on this day, for example, Mal was thinking it would be really cool to go pick daisies together. Is there even a badge for that?

"Goodness Grace Paley," Mal groaned to herself as she pulled on her jean jacket and quickly combed her fingers through her hair. "I'm the cheesiest person alive. I'm the cheesiest person alive and . . ."

3

Mal paused, staring at the spot where normally there would be socks.

"What the Gunta Stölzl?!"

"What's up?" Molly asked from inside her green shirt, which was almost over her head.

"Uh." Mal got down on her knees, searching her drawer with her fingers and coming up empty. "Wow. Seriously? NO SOCKS, like NONE?"

As of recently, socks and thinking about socks had become a very significant part of Mal's life. Which was surprising, because Mal was more into flannel and collector pins (and buttons) than socks.

At first it seemed like Mal had an abundance of socks. Then, recently, a closer examination revealed that what Mal had was actually a lot of left socks.

Then even Mal's right socks—which, really, who can tell the difference?—started disappearing.

Now, disappearing had become officially DISAPPEARED.

Molly searched the floor, then bent over and picked up a single Mal sock. "Here's one! That's a start? Or, you know, a foot."

Of course, one sock is hardly a victory when you need two.

Mal and Molly hunted and pecked around Roanoke cabin for almost half an hour, while the rest of Roanoke waited in the mist outside.

"We need to do laundry so Mal can borrow OUR socks," April said, tugging on the bow in her hair and channeling their incredibly responsible counselor, Jen.

"Alternately, Mal could switch to sandals," Jo, who was always coming up with solutions, and preferred sensible boots and wool socks, suggested.

"You can't have adventures in *sandals*," April scoffed, because April was always thinking about adventures. "They're OPEN TOE."

Roanoke cabin's friend Barney, who was very much for a stylish sandal but was also very pro-safety, would agree.

"I'm sure plenty of people adventure in sandals," Jo said. "I'm sure people do lots of things in sandals."

A very huge grin spread over April's face. "They could solve a mystery . . . if something was AFOOT!"

Jo paused, soaking in the first pun of the morning. "Right."

Ripley bounced in place, ready for her morning waffles, her blue hair winking in the sun. "You could have a BEACH adventure. Then you could wear flip-flops or no flops and just have TOES."

"Except, Mal plus water equals—" April made an X with her arms.

In the end, Molly lent Mal a pair of her socks, a sparkly yellow-and-white-striped pair with bumble bees on them and MOLLY written clearly on the bottom of the right toe.

5

"I like you in sparkly socks." Molly grabbed Mal's hand as they made their way to the mess hall, trailing behind the others.

Mal hooked her arm over Molly's shoulder. "I'll try not to lose them."

"It's okay if you do," Molly said. "I'm not super sock oriented or anything."

Mal stepped into the noisy mess hall. "I feel like socks have weirdly become like the mystery of my life! Like, SOCKS, you know?"

April poked her head between the two of them. "I just wanted to say, your socks are the BEE'S KNEESOCKS!"

Molly rolled her eyes.

"The bee's TOES!" Ripley corrected, grabbing the syrup.

Jo watched as Ripley began stacking what would eventually be a tower of twenty pancakes onto her plate.

Mal grabbed a fork. "Looks like it's shaping up to be a record-breaking kind of day."

"I'm gonna put all these in my belly!" Ripley cheered.

And then, miraculously, given her size, which was not much taller than a stack of twenty pancakes, Ripley did just that.

It was one of a few awesome things to happen that day, but it was pretty awesome.

Just as Ripley folded her final forkful into her face, there was the familiar clomp of Rosie's stride to the front of the room.

"Listen up, scouts!" Rosie bellowed. "Myself and Counselor Jenae—"

"Jen," Jen corrected, without missing a beat.

Rosie continued. "—have a big announcement!"

April jumped up from her seat. "WHAT THE REBECCA SUGAR! RIPLEY JUST ATE TWENTY PANCAKES!"

"Fabulous." Rosie pulled out the giant mail sack. "Also. Mail's here."

In an effort to achieve some level of consistency with the mail, Camp Director Rosie had recently turned all the postage-related responsibilities over to SPARKLE FORCE, a troupe of former scouts who ran special ops tactical maneuvers and rhythm and movement classes for active seniors.

As a result, for the moment, the mail was on time.

Rosie pulled out the first letter while Jen held the sack open. "Listen up for your name to be called."

The bag was covered in what looked like pearly white sand, which Rosie didn't explain, and Jen didn't ask about, because sometimes you have to save up your questions for the big things. The bag was also full of packages and, by some strange coincidence, there was a package for every member of Roanoke.

"APRIL!" got a set of puffy unicorn stickers from her favorite aunt and a new set of fountain pens from her dad.

"Finally," April sighed, "I can make my MARK! Get out a little bit of this PENt up creativity."

"We get it," Mal said.

"JO!" got a teeny-tiny screwdriver that looked like it should maybe be for an elf or a faerie but was actually for people who liked to take really tiny things apart, like Jo.

"Hey, it's A MINI DRIVER!" April boomed. "GET IT?!"

"RIPLEY!" got a MASSIVE box of peanut butter and hot pepper cookies, her mom's secret recipe.

"MAL!"

Mal dug greedily into her package. Mal's mom always sent the coolest things. Sometimes she sent cookies from Mal's grandma, which were often covered in cat hair (from her grandma's dozen cats) but pretty good once you got the fuzz off. Today it was sheet music for Mal and Molly's now pretty decent accordion trio, which still didn't have a name, and a box of caramel corn.

"MOLLY!"

Isn't it amazing how a seemingly possibly good day can turn in the same amount of time it takes a cat to scratch, which is not a lot of time?

Amazing is probably the wrong word.

It's actually more of a bummer.

9

Molly looked at the package Jen had placed in front of her, covered in neat rows of stamps. She bit her lip.

The box was wrapped in thick brown paper and tied with string. It weighed slightly more than a box of rocks.

"What is it?" Mal asked, leaning over to see.

Molly sighed, melting down onto the table. "It's from my mom."

CHAPTER 2

Here are things that are fun to get in a package:

Lollipops
Hiking equipment
Comic books
Letters from home
Pictures of kittens
Stickers
Socks
Brownies/cookies

Also acceptable:

Band-Aids
Your allergy medication
Sunscreen

More clothing labels

Batteries

Insect repellant

Oatmeal packets

These things can always be shipped in generous quantities so they can be shared and bartered as needed.

Clearly Molly's mom was not aware of this basic package protocol.

Mal watched as Molly gingerly pulled on the twine holding the bundle together, twisted with one of her mother's infamously impenetrable knots.

"Is it socks?" Mal asked hopefully.

"I doubt it." Molly peeled back the thick construction paper, her expression pickled into a sour grimace Mal only saw when Molly got word from home.

The package was full of thin blue exercise books, all labeled MOLLY and covered in Post-it notes with detailed instructions like "Complete me first," "Concentrate, Molly," and "Try to focus and not get distracted, as is your habit."

Mal wrinkled her nose. "What is that? Is that a Post-it note? Is that MANY Post-it notes?"

It is well known that IF you are going to send homework to someone at camp, which you should not do, the ratio of homework to candy or something fun should be no greater than 1:12.

That means for every PAGE of homework you send, you should send twelve other really cool things (see list above).

Almost no one JUST sends homework to camp.

Because it's called HOMEwork.

Not CAMPwork.

Or CAMPfun.

But, as Molly's mother's Post-it notes explained, Molly was expected to use at least some of her time at camp to improve her chances of getting better grades at school the following year.

It should not be suggested that Molly was a bad student. Even Jo knew that not especially liking math does not a bad student make.

(Please note that the sending of books to people at camp is highly encouraged. THIS is a book. Books are awesome.)

Mal watched Molly sink into her seat, like someone was slowly releasing all the Molly out of Molly right in front of Mal's very eyes.

Without thinking, Mal snatched the package. She wanted to erase it.

Molly sighed another long, slow sigh. Like she was suddenly the most tired person.

"So, I guess . . ." She scratched her head. "Um, what are we doing now?"

"We . . ." Mal tucked Molly's unwelcome package under her arm. "WE are going to go have a wicked Lumberific day."

"You said it." April nodded. April was always up for Lumberificness.

"My stomach kind of hurts, but yeah," Ripley said, dabbing at the syrup on her face.

"Seems like a good day for it," Jo chimed in.

"Sure." Molly sighed once again. "Okay."

April looked at Jo, who looked at Ripley, who was looking at Molly. Bubbles, Molly's trusty pet raccoon, who also liked to sleep on her head like a hat, climbed down from his perch on Molly's head and pressed his little furry face against her forehead.

"Squirp!" he chirped.

"Thanks, Bubbs," Molly said.

Mal frowned.

No, she thought. NO. A stupid package is not going to ruin Molly's day!

It would be fixed. MAL would fix it.

"Come on," she said, hooking Molly's arm. "I have an idea."

CHAPTER 3

Where do bad days come from? Why are some days bad and others good?

Despite extensive research by many smart people, the science on bad days is sketchy at best.

It is, scientists might say, pending further research.

There are some people who think bad days are caused by black cats. Black cats would like it to be known that they have plenteous good days and they are in no way responsible for your mom's car getting towed or any of that other stuff. There are also people who think stepping on cracks causes bad days. Cracks in the sidewalk would like you to know that they are trip hazards, sure, but not responsible for you dropping your ice cream or any of that other stuff.

What was clear to Mal was that something in Molly's package had made the rest of the day irreparably, irretrievably BAD.

Even though Molly left the books under Mal's bed in Roanoke cabin, it was like she was lugging them around everywhere she went. Through everything she and Mal did that day, it was like she was carrying them in her soul.

Or something.

A bad thing happening can feel like a push through a trapdoor that sends you tumbling down into a rotten day. That's why people say things like "It all went downhill from there." Because sometimes a bad day is like riding backward on a wagon with three different-size wheels down a hill made of angry rocks.

Also, watching someone you care about so so so much have a bad day can feel pretty horrible.

And so.

Mal's first solution to Molly's bad-day vibes was to take her to the archery range, because Mal knew Molly was a great archer, and doing something you're great at is sometimes a way to feel good.

Or better.

But after her first shot, Molly's string broke and then her arrow broke and then Molly didn't feel like shooting anymore.

"Okay," Mal said, rubbing her hands together. "Okay. No problem. What about, um, music?"

Molly was a much better musician than she might ever give herself credit for. Which made music something that generally made Molly feel good. Generally.

But that day, Molly sat slumped over her accordion. No matter what keys she put her fingers on, they were the wrong keys. It was like the wrong keys were jumping out of place and sliding under her fingertips.

"I can't do this," Molly groaned, dropping her head on the accordion, which generated a loud WEEEEEEZE sound.

That made Bubbles put his little paws over his ears.

"It's okay." Mal unstrapped her accordion. "We don't have to play music we can . . . um."

Mal looked around. What was a guaranteed anti–bad day thing to do?

If Molly was Ripley, Mal could just dip her in glitter, but Molly was not Ripley.

"It's fine," Molly said, standing up slowly, like someone with a head cold. "It's lunch, so . . . let's just go to the mess."

You would actually think lunch would be a pretty safe place to avoid a bad day. And it was . . . until Molly accidentally stuck her elbow in a plate of guacamole.

"Great," Molly grumbled.

I mean, it was that really good, super creamy, Kzyzzy special HOLY MOLY VEGAN GUACAMOLE.

Mal held her breath.

April reached for a napkin. "It's okay, Mol," she chirped. "It's just avocado and what I'm guessing is a hint of tofu mayo."

"Whatever." Molly watched the green goop drip off her elbow. "I'm sure my elbow will enjoy it."

"You can still eat that," Ripley pointed out, handing Bubbles a chip.

Bubbles, among many other things, was a raccoon who LOVED guacamole.

"Thanks, Rip," Molly said, holding out her sleeve while Bubbles carefully scraped off a good-size serving.

"It's okay," she said quietly when Bubbles was finished. "I wasn't really hungry."

"What do I do?" Mal hissed while Molly headed to put her tray away.

"With what?" Jo asked.

"With this . . ." Mal checked to see if Molly was in earshot. "BAD DAY?"

"Scientifically speaking," Jo said, finishing the last of her chips, "there's not much you can do. In my understanding, research is still pending."

Mal pressed her fingers together. "Maybe nothing else bad will happen?"

Jo knew there was no scientific theory that said there were a finite number of bad things that can happen to a person in a given day.

Bad days aren't like prime numbers, lovely reliable prime numbers.

Bad days, if they are really good bad days, can always get worse. In fact, they often have a pinnacle, a height of bad day, a pièce de résistance of BLEH, basically a moment where you can sit back and go, "WOW, this is a REALLY bad day."

For Molly, this moment transpired while she and Mal and Ripley were picking herbs for their Herb in the Hand badge.

Mal thought this activity might help because the herb garden in question was tucked in the forest, so it meant going into the woods, which was a place that usually made Molly happy.

It did.

But then while Molly was picking scallions she started thinking about the salads she used to make in her backyard, when she was little, out of grass and the tops of the radishes from her mother's garden. Which used to drive her mom nuts.

"MOLLY!" her mother would shriek from the back porch, hands on hips. "What are you doing picking WEEDS?"

Sometimes it felt like the only time Molly's parents noticed her was when she was doing something they thought was wrong.

"Hey, Molly," Ripley called back, holding up a handful of basil, "are you feeling better?"

"What?" Molly stepped out of the garden, looking back at Ripley. "Did you ask for something, Rip—"

Just then, Molly's toe caught on a rock, and she fell forward, swirling past Ripley, who was bent over smelling some leaves.

"Molly!" Mal cried out, dropping the dill she'd gathered.

Molly spun on her right foot, tripped over another branch, scraped past a pine tree and, finally, landed with what could be described as a tremendous SPLOOSH in a giant puddle of mud.

"Great Lucy Maud Montgomery!" Mal ran over. "Are you okay?"

Molly sighed her longest sigh of the day. It took about a minute to get the whole thing out. She looked at her muddy palms. "Good thing Bubbles is off at dance class."

Mud dripped down Molly's cheek, down the back of her neck, and flooded her sneakers.

"Here." Mal held out her hand. "I'll get you out."

Mal grabbed Molly's hand and heaved. But Molly did not move.

"Or I could just stay in the mud," Molly grumbled. "Forever."

It ended up taking Ripley and Mal and Veronica from Dartmoor to pull Molly out of the puddle with a somewhat satisfying SMUCK.

Standing next to the puddle, Molly held her arms out and looked down. "I look like . . ."

"A mud wrestler," Ripley said, because that's what Molly looked like.

"A really cool mud wrestler," Mal added, because it was clear Molly did not want to look like a mud wrestler.

"Great," Molly said. Her shoes squitched. She had mud in her ear. And her nose. And her mouth.

"At least . . ." Mal said, searching her brain for something to say that was good about being muddy. There were a few good things, actually. "You got a free mud mask!"

Molly ran a finger over her gritty cheek. "Hooray," she said, unconvinced.

"Come on." Mal put her arm over Molly's shoulder. "Let's go back to camp."

The score, for those keeping track, was:

Bad day: 4.

Mal: 0.

But the day wasn't over.

Yet.

CHAPTER 4

It seems appropriate to mention one good thing about bad days.

Which is that, even though they can get worse, they also MUST, absolutely, end.

No matter what missteps or misadventures take place in any given day, at the end of that day, no matter what, the sun will tuck itself below the horizon and send up some version of the moon into the sky.

That's not exactly how it works, of course.

But you get the idea.

Mal was relieved that this very weird, not-at-all-amusing day was about to end as she flopped down on her bed and waited for Molly to get changed out of her mud-soaked clothes.

"Hey, you know what?" she said, flipping through the comic on her bed. "Tomorrow is another day."

"Yes," Molly said, pulling on a clean sweater and crawling down from her bunk. "That is true."

Molly sat down on Mal's bunk. "Do you ever think about that?"

"About what?" Mal asked.

"Nothing," Molly said. "Never mind."

In this case, both "Never mind" and "Nothing" were actually referring to the thought Molly often had that every end of a day was a day at camp she wouldn't get back. The thought that there were only so many days of summer left, even though it seemed like this summer was way longer than any summer Molly could remember. But all summers end, all of them, and every day that went by was a day closer to going . . . home.

Home, where homework and her mother's Post-it notes were a huge part of every day, instead of just a small package stashed under the bed.

Mal took Molly's hand in hers. Mal knew Molly well enough that she could tell when Molly was thinking about going home, something that Mal knew made Molly scared and a little sad. When Molly was thinking about home, she looked smaller. Like she was trying to take up less space.

When you care about someone, you don't want them to feel small. You want them to feel like a big sparkling star. You want them to feel like a giant colorful hot-air balloon of a person.

"Hey." Mal stood up. "What do you say we go and roast marshmallows by a giant, but carefully constructed by Barney, campfire?"

The campfire was Mal's last hope for the day. She was really really hoping that a toasted marshmallow would act like some sort of magic spell.

This is asking a lot of a marshmallow. But it is possible. Depending on the marshmallow and how you toast it.

While Molly sat on a log with April and Jo and Ripley, Mal picked what looked like the best marshmallow from the bag and went to find the perfect stick to toast the perfect marshmallow. Fortunately, Mal knew the perfect stick finder.

"I bequeath you this stick," Jo said, handing over the perfect long, thin, and sturdy oak twig she kept for just such an occasion, "to combat Molly's unfortunate day."

The key to good marshmallow roasting is, first, location. You find your coal and that's your coal. It should be a little glowing red and a little white. You want it to be in an uncrowded area.

Then it's all patience.

As the skin of Molly's marshmallow, toasted by Mal, reached the perfect brown, the brown all marshmallow toasters strive for that is somewhere between mocha and caramel, Zodiac stepped up to the fire and, in unison, held out their flashlights.

GHOST STORY TIME!

"OKAY, SCOUTS," sneered "Skulls" Mackenzie of Zodiac cabin, twisting her cap backward, "LET'S GET SCARED!"

"Mal!" Molly cried out, pointing.

Mal turned just in time to see Molly's marshmallow burst into flames.

CHAPTER 5

A fire is a very cozy, enchanted kind of place, especially a roaring bonfire surrounded by scouts. It's something about the light. Something to do with the smell of kindling and smoke and the leftover traces of the day still lingering in the night air.

As the Lumberjanes' resident theater director and commentator on all things dramatic, Annabella Panache, would say, it is the ideal stage for a storyteller to spin their web.

Which is fitting, because the storyteller taking the stage was Wren of Zodiac cabin, who happened to be wearing a big spiderweb on her sweater. Because Wren liked things that were a little bit creepy, and spiders, among the many things they are, are also that.

While Mal watched Molly gingerly chewing her charcoal-coated marshmallow, Wren stepped up to the fire.

"I submit to you scouts and phantoms," she said in a creaky, creepy voice, "a story that's sure to put ice in your veins and . . . worms in your spaghetti."

"Worms!" Jo shuddered, because worms really creeped Jo out.

Wren clicked on her flashlight and held it under her chin. "A story of the most haunted spot in all of Miss Qiunzella Thiskwin Penniquiqul Thistle Crumpet's Camp for Hardcore Lady-Types. The story of . . ."

Wren paused for dramatic effect.

. . .

Ripley popped another marshmallow in her mouth and cozied in between Jo and April.

The fire crackled.

"GHOST CABIN!" Wren's eyes blazed.

"Ghost Cabin." Molly looked up from her marshmallow, a little bit of black stuck to her bottom lip.

Mal raised an eyebrow.

"GHOOOOST Cabin!" The flashlight flickered under Wren's chin. "A wholly haunted habitation in which dwell spirits that stalk campers in the black of night . . ."

Ripley's eyes were as big as pie plates as she licked the last of her marshmallow off her fingers.

Bubbles, who had managed to secure a marshmallow of his own, chirped nervously.

"The ghosts of Ghost Cabin are here, in the shadows of the places familiar by day but strange in darkness." Wren's voice fell to a whisper.

"You can feel them, wisps of air, mysterious frosty breezes," Wren hissed, a convenient ripple of breeze wafting through the campfire, causing the flames to flash and cast shadows around the scouts, now transfixed.

"You can hear them"—Wren's voice dropped even lower—"sneaking through your cabins, ghostly bodies hiding in plain sight, crying out in the night . . ."

"GIVE US YOUR SOCKS!" Hes screamed, jumping out from behind the rows of scouts, a ghost sock puppet on each hand.

All scouts in attendance jumped off the log with a sudden JOLT.

"WHAT THE SHIRLEY JACKSON?!" Jo cried.

April, who did not like ghost stories much, as she did not really believe in ghosts, grabbed her chest. "HOLY HEART (the band) ATTACK!"

"Ghosts," Molly said.

Mal, who could not hear because a very freaked-out raccoon named Bubbles had launched onto her face in a fit of fear, let out a muffled, "What did you say?"

"Ghosts!" Molly repeated, her eyes suddenly alight. "What if it's GHOSTS?"

CHAPTER 6

After a good scare, Barney, who was always very considerate, thought it would be nice to soothe everyone's nerves with chamomile-and-lavender-infused cupcakes, handed out by Barney, Kzyzzy the cook, and BunBun, the very serious daughter of Kzyzzy.

"Take your cupcake," BunBun said, holding out her tray.

The green glow-in-the-dark pom-poms on BunBun's head made her look even more like a cool alien than usual. Also, she had a goopy moustache of blue icing, which looked sort of on purpose, because it curled up at the ends in kind of a fancy way.

Ripley reached forward to grab a cupcake. BunBun pulled back the tray.

BunBun pointed at the cupcake in question. "This one is NOT your cupcake. This one is Jo's."

"Okay," Ripley said, pulling back her hand. "Which one is mine?"

"THIS one. This one is for the ghost," BunBun said, pointing to one in the corner of the tray. "Don't eat it."

Ripley carefully plucked her cupcake off the tray and BunBun moved on, her boppers bopping in the wind.

The rest of Roanoke was still avidly discussing Wren's ghost story and its connection to Mal's socks.

"Maybe it's just made-up," April offered. "For instance, the Lemonade Stand book *Make-Up Your Mer-Mind* suggests that mermaids struggle with decisions, but I don't think that's true."

April's experience with mermaids, while limited, suggested that they were pretty cool and liked rocking out. But it's good to note that any experience you have with a magical creature is just one experience and not enough to come to a general conclusion about a group, magical or not.

April was more a fan of mermaids than she was of ghosts, so she was hoping maybe someone else would like to spend some more time talking about mermaids.

"Maybe ghosts just like socks," Molly said.

"Do ghosts have feet that they would need socks for?" Jo wondered.

35

Ripley wiped a dot of icing off her chin. "People have feet. I mean. Not all people, but some people."

Jo pointed at Ripley as if to say, "You have a point there." Which she would have said if she wasn't chewing on a cupcake. Because chewing with her mouth open was something Jo thought was kind of rude.

April was less concerned about chewing with her mouth open.

She leaned back on her log, her toes to the fire, mouth chomping. "Is it just me or does this cupcake taste like a really fluffy flower?"

"Why would ghosts want MY socks?" Mal asked, munching, brow furrowed. "April has nicer socks. Ripley has TOE socks."

"I love toe socks! It's a mini sock for each toe!" Ripley cheered. "My toe socks are in the laundry."

"Maybe it's a coincidence that it's your socks," Molly said. "Maybe they're coming for our socks NEXT."

Previous to this summer, Mal was never one to care about socks. At home, socks were something her mom folded into little squares and put in her drawer, because it was something her mom liked to do, and if she didn't, Mal had a tendency to just stuff them all in her drawer so it looked like a drawer of swirling sock snakes.

It's one thing to care about your socks, it is another to be in the middle of a sock situation.

Still.

Mal couldn't help but notice that since they'd started talking about ghosts and socks, Molly had stopped looking sad. Now she looked like she was thinking.

Molly took a nibble of her cupcake. "Maybe there's a folk reference somewhere that talks about ghosts and socks or ghosts and a general connection to fiber arts."

Hes plopped down next to Roanoke with a grin from ear to ear. "So? Were you freaked? It was scary, right? You guys were totally bugged out!"

Ripley held the hand that wasn't holding her cupcake to her chest. "I can still feel my heart beating!"

"Where did you come up with the socks thing?" Molly asked, leaning over Mal.

"Oh." Hes shrugged, as this was the less interesting thing about the campfire story to her. "The socks thing was Wren's idea. BUT the scaring-the-goose-down-out-of-you-guys thing . . ." Hes folded her arms over her chest, tucking her sock puppets, still on her hands, under her arms. "THAT was MY IDEA!"

Hes stood up and bounded over to the next group of people, to make sure they were also really scared.

37

Mal looked over at Molly, who was munching quietly and looking at the flames. "It's kind of a cool sock MYSTERY," she said.

"Yeah." Molly smiled, the orange and red of the bonfire reflected in her eyes. "I read a book about a ghost that took a woman's hair ribbons. I can't remember what happened. But it was my favorite ghost story. 'The Case of the Missing Bow.' "

Mal closed her eyes, feeling the warm flames on her face. "Well, I'm glad you feel better."

It was time for bed. Scouts wandered off, leaving the warmth of the fire for their cabins.

Barney and a helpful trio of scouts approached with buckets of water to make sure the fire was completely out before everyone went to bed.

The sound of sizzling flames filled the firepit as a less than perfect day was saved by sugar and fire.

In the cabin, while April and Jo were trying to think of their scariest stories ("The Haunted Telescope!" "The Impact of the Patriarchy!"), Mal kicked off her now only pair of socks and left them curled up on the floor like snails.

"GOOD NIGHT, EVERYBODY!" Ripley hollered, curled up on her bunk. "HOPE NO ONE HAS SCARY DREAMS!"

"Geez." Jo curled up in her covers. "Now that you mention it . . ."

"GOOD NIGHT, RIPLEY," April hollered back.

Jo reached out and clicked off the light.

"Boo!" someone whispered in the darkness.

"Ha ha," Mal scoffed, thinking it was Molly. "Very funny. You'd better not be stealing my socks, *ghost*."

And then she closed her eyes and fell into a deep, marshmallow-filled sleep.

CHAPTER 7

The next morning Jo and Ripley woke up early and headed to the lake for a safety seminar with Seafarin' Karen and Barney, as part of their Water Safety RULES! badge.

April, who already had this badge, was off to get her SNAP! badge for photography.

Molly headed toward the kitchen to work on her Maki Me a Believer badge with sushi master BunBun.

Mal was supposed to join Hes and Barney's rugby team for practice, but . . .

"AW, COME ON!"

Mal stood in the middle of the cabin. "Where did they GO?!"

Now even Molly's sparkly bee socks were gone.

"Unless . . ." Mal climbed up to peek at Molly's bed. No socks, but there was a sleeping raccoon curled up around . . .

Mal peered closer. Bubbles's little claws gripped the edge of a large, imposing-looking textbook covered in Post-its.

"What the Ada Lovelace," Mal said. She'd thought she'd seen Molly reading something early that morning, but she'd hoped she was reading something cool.

Poor Molly, Mal thought, doing HOMEWORK when she should be at her Molly LumberBEST.

Later, on the rugby pitch, while half of her brain was ready to play for Team Barney, at least three-quarters of Mal's brain (the math is a work in progress) couldn't stop worrying about Molly.

"She got MATH homework at CAMP? I love math, but that is super uncool," Hes said, handing Mal a pair of socks on the edge of the rugby pitch.

"That explains why she was feeling so un-Molly-like yesterday," Barney added. "I mean, it's one thing to do math because you LOVE math. It's another thing entirely to have math thrust upon you."

"My mom sent me almond brittle." Hes grinned. "And crossword puzzles!"

Mal slipped on her sneakers. Hes's feet were about two sizes bigger than hers, so the socks bunched up around her ankles.

But they were socks.

"OKAY, SCOUTS," Jen tweeted from the center of the pitch. "LET'S PLAY RUGBY!"

Easier said than done. Mal couldn't concentrate. Even with a wall of determined Dartmoor scouts rushing toward her, Mal had a serious case of "What about Molly?" brain.

"Molly deserves to have FUN," she fumed, darting across the pitch, next to Barney.

"Of course," Barney said, tossing the ball to Mal. "Everyone deserves to have fun!"

"It's just that she starts thinking about this stuff, this home stuff and . . ." Mal tucked the ball under her arm and huffed it to the goal line. "And she gets all sad."

"Well—" Barney started to say that the best thing they could do was be supportive, but then Alicia from Dartmoor jumped and tackled Barney to the ground. "GUH!"

"RUN, MAL!" Hes cried from the other end of the field. "MAL! RUN!"

"Yeek!" Mal jumped and sprinted up the field.

Mal was fast, but Dartmoor was faster. Haley Court, Dartmoor's most vicious forward, jumped up in the air like

43

a tiger, soared over her fellow teammates, and tackled Mal so hard that she punched the ball out from under Mal's arm. It sailed into the air and into the awaiting arms of Hes.

"HA HA!" Hes bolted up the pitch, ball in arm.

Mal laid on the ground. Thinking.

What if Molly needed a distraction, Mal thought. Something to take up the space the package was holding in her brain.

Molly needed . . .

"OF COURSE!" Mal popped up from the ground and brushed the dirt off her knees.

"HEY!" Mal danced over to Barney, who was still recovering from their tackle. "If Molly has something ELSE to think about, something to FIGURE OUT, then she won't have any space in her brain left to think about her mom's package and be sad."

"Oh." Barney wondered if that would work.

Mal was sure it would.

So sure that she forgot she was playing rugby and took off running to the mess hall, where the air was thick with the smell of maki rice and soy sauce.

"Hey." Mal spotted Molly at the corner table, neatly slicing rows of rolled sushi with a knife as big as her arm.

The pieces of cucumber maki Molly was cutting up looked like little minus and plus signs laid out on a plate decorated with edible pink flowers.

44

"They're Math Maki," Molly explained. "You want to try one?"

"Better question." Mal waggled her eyebrows, picking up a plus sign from the plate. "Are YOU hungry for a MYSTERY?!"

Molly looked confused. "Mystery Maki?"

"No! My socks," Mal explained. "They're missing. Again. Your socks! And I thought maybe today we could figure out what happened. I mean, do you want to . . . investigate?"

Molly rolled her eyes. "Hungry for a mystery? You're hilarious. Does my mystery come with a side of wasabi?"

Seeing Molly smile, Mal felt an instant flood of relief. This was a perfect idea.

"No, but it comes with . . ." Mal considered, grabbing another maki and popping it in her mouth. "Um. SOCK-I?"

"Holy Hiromi Goto, that's a bad pun." Molly burst into laughter. "Okay, let's go."

CHAPTER 8

Mal and Molly agreed that their first step should be to talk to Wren, who they found sitting at a picnic table under a tall pine in the main courtyard.

Wren was editing her ghost story, which can be the longest part of writing a ghost story; a process that involves writing things down on a pad of paper, feeling really good, then rereading what you wrote and crossing everything out. Repeat.

Wren's skin was so pale that, in the moonlight, Molly had often thought that Wren looked a little like a ghost. In the sunlight, she looked like she needed sunscreen.

Wren was worried her story wasn't spooky enough. "I don't want to rely on theatrics," she told Mal and Molly, pushing her purple hair off her face. "I want it to be legit spooky, you know? On paper."

"Maybe the ghosts could eat the socks," Mal offered, "then you can talk about teeth, and teeth are super spooky."

Wren chewed on her pencil. "Maybe," she said. "I'm thinking of a new title, 'Ghoulish Apparitions Dwell Here.' What do you think?"

47

"I thought 'Ghost Cabin' was a pretty good title. Where did you get, you know, the idea," Molly asked, "for the socks and the ghosts?"

Wren thought for a second. "Um. Barney told us about the missing socks, because they're knitting you new socks."

"Aw, that's so sweet!" Mal clasped her hands together.

"Yeah, then I remembered Vanessa telling us something about a ghost cabin," Wren added. "And . . . then I put all that together in my story."

"Interesting," Mal said.

"So." Molly raised a finger. "Now we talk to Vanessa!"

Vanessa was the Zodiac cabin counselor and she had the best hair in camp. When Mal and Molly found her, she was finishing up her barber skills workshop for scouts working on their Shave the Way badge and gliding a wide broom over the black-and-white tiles of the Lumberjanes barbershop, the Big Clipper.

"Do *you* remember who told *you* the story of Ghost Cabin?" Molly asked.

Mal checked her fade in the mirror. "Hmmmm."

Vanessa sighed, kicking the hair off her boots. "Geez, that was so long ago. Maybe ask Jen?"

"Before we go, can I get a quick fade fix?" Mal asked, pointing at her slightly too-long left side.

Mal and Molly found Jen at the top of the beach, weighed down with life preservers from Barney's water safety seminar "102 Reasons to Wear a Life Preserver." Jen was not fond of ghost stories, mostly because she had been told, several times, that her stories were either not scary at all or WAY TOO SCARY.

"Ghost Cabin? I don't think so." Jen held up the life jackets with a hopeful smile. "Are you scouts here to learn about life preservers?"

Molly shook her head. "We're kind of working on this ghost story thing."

"Ghost story?" Rosie strode up from the water's edge, a handful of floppy kelp in one hand and, mysteriously, an anchor in the other. "Someone asking about ghosts?"

"Oh, us," Mal said, kicking sand out of the sandals she'd changed into.

"We are," Molly added. "As it relates to socks. And general ghost curiosity. And socks."

"Well, curiosity is a good thing," Rosie said, shaking the sand out of her kelp.

"So." Molly's eyes got wide. "Do you know anything about . . ."

It seemed very unlikely that Rosie would spill any information about anything, but it was worth trying.

Rosie smiled.

"I'll leave you to it," she said, and with a sharp nod, she strode off with her kelp and anchor, leaving a trail of drips in her wake. Rosie had a way of making it seem like she was going to say something while actually not saying something. There is no badge for this skill . . . yet.

Jen, who was relieved not to have heard yet another version of her name, went off to make sure that as many scouts as possible knew about water safety.

"This is a bit of a wild-ghost chase," Molly said.

"Hey!" Vanessa appeared through the trees, a bag full of clippers in her arms. "I just thought of something, about the ghost story. I don't know if I told Wren this . . ."

Molly and Mal looked on expectantly. "Yes?"

Vanessa shifted the clippers to prevent them from falling. "So, there was a lake that the Ghost Cabin was supposed to be on."

"A lake." Mal's stomach flipped. "Really?"

"Yeah, it was . . ." Vanessa mused. "Goddess, this was so long ago. My brain! It was called . . ."

Vanessa, as older people sometimes do, trailed off and into the corners of her mind. Thinking.

Vanessa snapped her fingers, causing the many chains around her wrists to jingle. "LAKE SPECTER! You know, like INspector, but a lake, and spelled differently. With an *e*. I think . . . I think it's over past Wiggly Woods. Or Worm Woods. One of those."

Molly beamed. "That's super helpful! Thanks."

"*Lake* Specter." Mal sunk into the sand as Vanessa pivoted back to her counselor duties.

Molly put a hand on Mal's shoulder as she sank down next to her. "Aw, it's gonna be okay."

Mal looked off into the distance with a look that could easily be described as . . . haunted.

"Lakes." Mal sank into the sand. "Why did it have to be lakes?"

CHAPTER 9

One of the least checked-out books in Miss Qiunzella's giant library collection is a small black book with the title *Nelly Madison Robias's Giant Collection of Phobias.*

It is one of many books written by an alumna.

It is possible that Nelly Robias was destined to write this book because of her last name, or because she is on record as the scout with the most phobias in the entire history of scouts.

Nelly suffered from nephophobia (fear of clouds), koniophobia (fear of dust), anthophobia (fear of flowers), odontophobia (fear of dentistry), and a whole host of other things that have been collected in *Nelly Madison Robias's Giant Collection of Phobias* and so do not need to be repeated here.

Curiously, one thing Nelly was not afraid of was water (hydrophobia), which was a thing that Mal, who was not afraid of flowers, dentistry, dust, or clouds, was VERY VERY afraid of.

52

As a person afraid of water, Mal was also afraid of waves (cyrnophobia) and rivers (potamophobia), and she really did not enjoy pool toys and extensive discussion of bathing suits (although she would not classify these as actual fears).

As someone who cared about Mal a lot a lot, Molly knew that bodies of water were basically like big scary monsters to Mal (actually worse, because big scary monsters weren't such a big deal).

"It's okay," Molly said, patting Mal on the back with gentle loving pats. "We can make you socks. We can get our Sock It to Me badge!"

Mal looked down at her sandals. Mal knew that if April or Jo or Ripley were there, they would probably talk her into going to the lake.

Jo would say that, technically, being within the perimeter of a lake did not mean being in a lake and so it was nothing to be afraid of to just go TO a lake. ("Also, you're already on a BEACH now," Jo would point out.)

Ripley would bounce around and say maybe the lake would be fun, and a person should never turn down the possibility of doing something that could be exciting.

April would get that determined look on her face and say that the waters and the woods were there for exploring and discovering and would maybe quote something from a mermaid book.

But Molly wasn't doing any of those things, because Molly didn't care about a lake, she cared about Mal.

Because that's what Molly did, Mal thought, she cared about people. Other people. Like when people felt sad, Molly was always the first person to know the right thing to say.

Mal did not always know the right thing to say.

Mal looked up. "Do YOU want to go to Lake Specter?"

"Do *you*?" Molly asked reflexively.

"I'm asking you," Mal repeated, "if *you* want to. I mean, if I wasn't afraid, you would want to go, right?"

Molly twisted her lips. "Maybe. I mean, I'm curious. I mean . . . You know, it's a mystery."

"Okay. Let's go." Mal stood up and brushed the sand off her knees, her face set in a determined grimace.

"Really?" Molly raised an eyebrow. "To the *lake*?"

Mal considered. "Maybe it's a really very small lake? That's possible, for a lake to be very very small?"

"Sure," Molly said. Although generally, very very small lakes are called puddles, not lakes.

Either way, Mal thought, Molly was happy, which made Mal feel better. Lake or no.

Mal took Molly's hand. "Should we grab reinforcements?"

Molly nodded, and they headed off to the cabins. "I think, once again, this is a job for . . . ROANOKE!"

CHAPTER 10

By the time they got everyone together, the sun was low in the sky. It hadn't rained in days and the forest floor was prickly and dry. Cicadas chirped in the background as they headed through the trees, Ripley skipping ahead with Bubbles, April with the map, Jo with the compass, and Mal and Molly at the back, holding hands.

Molly breathed in the warm summer air. "Pines," she sighed.

"I thought Wiggly Woods would be more wiggly!" Ripley chirped.

"Well, you're very wiggly," Mal said, "so you can make up for the general lack of wiggliness."

"On it," Ripley called back as she snaked through the trees.

"It's funny," Jo noted, looking up. "No matter how far we go in every direction, there's always something new to discover around here."

April checked her map. "Because Lumberjanes are ALWAYS exploring! So. According to this, we continue due west. At least that's the direction that seems to cut most directly through this particular forest."

"Is there a lake coming up?" Molly asked.

"There's a few," April noted, running her finger along their trail. "I'm thinking the little-bitty one here . . ." She pointed at a small blue blob. "Is probably Lake Specter. It's little-bitty so there's not a name on it, but I have a vibe."

Jo tipped her head to the side. "Do you really think ghosts took Mal's socks?"

This was something April had been wondering, so she chimed in, "Good question. I mean, I'm TOTALLY up for a mystery, OBVIOUSLY. But, I mean, it could also be that renegade squirrels took Mal's socks. Or renegade . . . grouses?"

"Renegade grouses?" Ripley peeked in from behind a tree. "Sneaking into houses?"

"I mean . . ." April wasn't sure how to say she didn't

think it was ghosts in a way that wouldn't stop the adventure she was also enjoying. "Maybe?"

"It could be," Molly said. "I mean, it could be a lot of things."

"Mind you," Mal added, "ghosts wouldn't be the weirdest phenomena we've come across here."

"The position of weirdest phenomena that we have come across," Jo said, "has yet to be filled."

"I am TOTALLY OKAY with pursing something based on a story, even if it is a ghost story," April stated. "I just wanted to say that, out loud. In case we do it again. Which I hope we do."

There were many fairy-tale creatures from her research that April was still hoping to run into.

Mal looked around. The brush was thick. Sort of endless. It was getting harder and harder to tell which way was the way forward and which way was just a step in a direction.

"What we need," Ripley said, "is a snack."

"What we need," Mal breathed into the hot summer air, "is a sign."

Which, as we've said many times, could be anything. But today, on this day, it was . . .

"LOOK!" Molly pointed up into a tree at a dangling,

57

relatively worse-for-the-wear sock clearly labeled on the bottom MAL.

"A sock," Ripley cheered.

"MY sock," Mal added.

"I'll get it!" Ripley hopped up from branch to branch and plucked the sock from the barb of the pine. "GOT IT!"

"Okay." April snapped to attention. "So we're on sock alert. Sock is GO repeat SOCK is GO, we are looking for socks now. Look high. Look low. Sock. Is. GO."

The socks were strung from the treetops of Wiggly Woods with care, in hopes, one would imagine, that someone would find them. Some clung to pine branches, a few were stuck to prickly berry bushes, one or two were laid out like sleeping slugs on rocks.

It was a tiny bit embarrassing, Mal thought, seeing her laundry laid out in the woods.

"Something put these socks out," Molly noted.

"I'm going to recall my suggestion that that something was a grouse," April said. "This does not seem grouselike."

"Maybe it could be a bunch of grouses stacked one on top of each other?" Ripley offered.

Ripley did a giant bounce and grabbed a sock from a relatively high tree branch. "Maybe something more bouncy?"

April stopped. "Is it weird that we've never considered it could be another scout? I mean, maybe this is Hes's act two?"

Ripley looked up at the branches. "No way. Barney has too much respect for socks for them to do something like this."

"True," Jo said. "Also, I feel like it's just SO unscoutly, you know?"

"Hey! This probably means we're getting close." Molly pointed at one sock stuck to a rock on the edge of a small brook.

"You know what else means we're getting close?" Ripley asked, pointing. "A lake."

Against her will, Mal let out a small noise that sounded a little like "Lake" and a little like "Oh no."

CHAPTER 11

Here is what some people might see when they see Lake Specter: a lake.

A person not afraid of bodies of water of all sizes might say that, on Lake Specter, sunlight dappled the water's surface.

A person not dealing with hydrophobia, like Ripley, might note that Lake Specter was full of fuzzy quacking ducklings and graceful geese, which, while vicious in nature, are not really scary, per se.

To a person not afraid of lakes, like April, Lake Specter might look like a lake from a movie with a castle and a princess, the kind of lake frequented by fairy creatures, who might gather to write poetry and eat dumplings made of leaves and giggles (a fairy delicacy).

A person not afraid of water, like Jo, might see Lake Specter as a great place to put a canoe, or an inflatable donut for floating on.

This is not what Mal saw when she saw Lake Specter.

The lake, to Mal, looked vast and ominous, which is a word you use for a place where you think something bad might happen.

When Mal looked at Lake Specter, something deep down below the water's surface looked back at her, something that would never ever be found.

As quietly as she could manage, Mal sucked in a deep, nervous breath.

"Do you want to turn around?" Molly whispered, grabbing Mal's hand. "I mean, you know, we found a bunch of your socks. So . . . ?"

Mal shook her head. "No, it's good. I'm fine. Really. You're having fun, right?"

"Sure," Molly said slowly.

"Then we're good." Mal smiled a quick stiff smile that showed all her teeth.

"So." Jo looked around. "Now what?"

"Now we observe!" Ripley noted.

"Good call, Rip!" April said, giving Ripley a chuck on the shoulder. "Observe we shall. What do we have here?"

Mal looked at the edge of the water. "Weird reeds reaching up like skinny green fingers, and rocks like grimy jagged teeth. Edge is slippery. You could slip on a rock and maybe slide into the cold water. Water is . . . muddy and dark with a green slime layer on top."

"Riiight." April, who had taken out her notebook, paused. "So. Creepy lake? I'm just writing 'creepy lake.'"

"Also, there's a bridge!" Jo noted, wandering over to the far west side of the lake's edge.

Mal would probably want it said that the bridge was a rickety, creepy-looking bridge. But she said nothing.

Molly, upon closer inspection, thought it looked solid enough, an arch built of wooden slats that were admittedly so coated in fuzzy green that it looked like the whole bridge was made out of moss.

"Why is everything close to a lake so SLIPPERY?" Mal moaned under her breath.

Molly put her left foot on the wooden bridge and pressed down. "I'll go first so you'll know it's safe."

"Does it feel stable?" April asked.

Molly stepped her right foot on the next slat and bounced ever so slightly. "Spongy. But, I think so."

Molly held her hand out to Mal. "Ready?"

Mal took a careful step, teeth gritted; the bridge felt like an old couch cushion under her feet.

Ripley, as Ripley often does, vaulted over with a quick bounce, followed by Jo and April.

The bridge connected to an island, which was really a cluster of rocks dotted with trees, pines, and bird poop.

"Lots of bird feces," Jo said.

Feces is a scientific word for poop.

"It is possible this whole island is bird poop," April said, making a note.

Ripley couldn't tell if this was supposed to be a good thing or a bad thing.

"It's fine," Mal whispered quietly to herself. "It's an island of poop. In a lake. This is fine. This is fi— HUAH!"

Molly turned around just in time to see Mal flip backward into a thicket of pines.

"Very slippery," Mal finished, on her back.

"Are you okay?" Molly called out, darting over rocks as she bolted toward Mal.

Mal's hand appeared from inside the trees. "YUP!"

There was a significant amount of rustling, then Mal's face burst through the thrush of green needles. "Guess what I found?"

"More socks?" Ripley asked.

"Better," Mal said, pulling back the branches. "A CABIN!"

CHAPTER 12

The cabin was about the same size as Mal's grandmother's toolshed, and somewhat hidden behind the long feathery branches of twisted pines that grew in the center of the island.

Whatever wood it was made of had wasted away to thin gray slats that barely touched, so you could see inside just by looking through the wall. The door, which might once have been white, but only shreds of paint remained, hung loosely on its last hinge, a rusted buckle that barely gripped the wood with a withered claw of a nail. The window was an empty grid except for a single jagged tooth of smoky glass that teetered in the frame.

Roanoke, with Ripley stacked on top of April and Bubbles squished on top of Jo, peeked through the door frame.

"Do we go in?" Mal asked.

"Looks abandoned," April said.

"We came all this way," Molly said, peering in. "And it doesn't feel like anyone's been here in a long time. Right? Are there Lumberrules for going into ghost cabins?"

"Probably," April reasoned. "I'm pretty sure there's a Lumberreason not to go into someone else's cabin without—"

Mal pointed. "MY SOCKS!"

There, in a neat pile in the middle of the cabin's single room, were several rows of stolen, folded socks. Green socks and blue socks. Orange socks. Superhero socks with lightning bolts on them.

"I feel like that's probable cause," April said, stepping inside.

"Wow." Ripley whistled, looking at the pile. "Mal, you have a lot of socks!"

"I mean, I DID. Geez." Mal kneeled next to the pile. "I guess I do now."

"So." Molly looked around. "I guess that solves part of the mystery. Except we still don't know WHO took them."

"Who took them and gave them back," Ripley added. "Do we think this is the sock stealer's house?"

Jo looked around the cabin. "You know, it looks small, but I think it's close to the same size as our cabin."

"No beds." Ripley pointed at the empty space next to the wall.

"If it's a ghost cabin," Molly wondered, "do ghosts need beds?"

"We still don't know it's a ghost," April pointed out, touching her finger to a dusty mirror that hung on one of the walls.

"Well, if it is ghosts . . ." Molly looked at the darkening skies outside the cabin door. "There's one way to find out."

Mal nodded. "We wait."

Jo leaned up against the wall. "It's going to take another hour for the sun to set. Get comfortable."

CHAPTER 13

In the dark, Lake Specter lived up to its name, Molly
thought.

At night, the lake was legit deep and creep: The dappled sunlight was replaced by the ominous, broken reflection of the crescent moon flickering on the water's surface,
the sweet lily pads now slick black holes. If Lake Specter
looked like a fairy tale during the day, at night it looked like
the opening scene of a nightmare.

Molly wasn't the only one with a bit of the creeps.

"Is it me," April asked, "or are there like three . . . four
unexplained creaks happening in this cabin right now?"

Jo looked up at the gaps between the ceiling beams. "I

think it's the wind. But I could be wrong. But I'm hoping I'm not."

Ripley wrapped her arms around herself. "It's cold!"

Mal looked at Molly, whose eyes seemed to be following some invisible thing around the room. "What are you looking at?"

"I don't know," Molly whispered. "I just felt something?"

"Is it a snoring raccoon on your head?" Mal asked.

Molly shook her head slowly. "That feeling I know. This is something else."

Just then, Mal felt what seemed like a tap on her back. Like someone had thrown a Cheeto at her.

Of course, no one had.

Jo pulled her flashlight out of one of her many pockets and pointed it into the darker corners of the cabin. The light grazed the soft gray surfaces, falling on nothing that looked suspicious to Jo. "Well, it's NIGHT now."

"Ghosts come out," Ripley whispered.

"Okay." April stood up. "It is REALLY cold."

The chill wasn't just cold, it was otherworldly. Unnatural. Like someone or something had dropped a giant ice cube into the cabin. Ripley shivered and pulled her sleeves down over her arms. Bubbles chirped and wrapped himself around Molly's neck.

WHOOOOOOOOOO

Jo, Mal, and Molly scrambled to their feet.
"Did you hear that?" Molly whispered.

WHOOOOOOOOOOOO

Ripley popped up and onto Jo's back. "I heard that."

WHOOOOOOOOO AAAAREEE

"Me too," Jo and April said together.
"Okay." Mal spun around. "Whoever that is, come out."
A shrill whistle. A whisper that bled into a shout.

WHOOOOOOOO AAARREEEE

CHAPTER 14

It has been difficult for Lumberresearchers to determine exactly when and where ghosts started saying "Boo."

Ghosts themselves are fairly mum on the subject, which is to say, ghosts have better things to do than to explain their word choices.

French ghosts, when they talk, don't say, "Boo." They say, "*Hou*," as in "*Hou* wants to know?" Except it's French, so that's actually not what they're saying. If they were, it would be "*Qui veut savoir?*"

There are some studiers of language who think that "Boo" was first used in Scotland as a word to scare children. No Scottish ghosts have confirmed this.

Probably a better question would be, why is the word "Boo," which is such a small word, so very scary when said by someone you think is a ghost?

Many scouts, including the members of Roanoke cabin, would guess it has more to do with the ghost part than the word part.

As Annabella Panache would say, "It's all in the delivery."

Outside the cabin, the night sounds of crickets and toads chirping were abruptly replaced by the crack of five harmonious Roanoke shrieks.

AAHHHHHHHHHHHHHHHHHHHH

Inside the cabin, as though she'd been shocked by a massive phantasmal charge, Mal shot up in the air. "GHOSTS!"

April stumbled backward. "ANGRY GHOSTS!"

Ripley grabbed on to Jo, who bolted out the door behind April, who was already on the tail of Mal and Molly, who was, once again, wrapped in Bubbles.

They soared over the bridge, not unlike a flock of flying fish or frisky unicorns.

They sped through Wiggly Woods, dodging trees like nimble kangaroos.

AHHHHHHHHHHHHH

Only when they saw the glow of the mess hall tent did April, Mal, Molly, Jo, and Ripley skid to a halt.

"Okay, so," Mal gasped, leaning on Molly. "The cabin. Was full. Of very upset ghosts."

"Ghosts are kind of scary when they creep up on you," Ripley wheezed. "AND THEN YELL 'BOO!'"

"What the Leslie Jones, you guys?!" April huffed.

"Many ghosts," Molly added, also out of breath. "So many ghosts. So many faces of dead people."

Jo walked to their cabin, still winded. "Which was to be expected, since that's what we were doing there. You know, waiting for ghosts. Still. Legitimately very scary."

April shoved her hands in her pockets. "Didn't think we would scream and sprint away like that. Given that we have seen many things that were scary."

Mal panted for breath. "Took us off guard. That's what happened. Took us. Off guard."

"Because it was still SURPRISE ghosts." Ripley nodded, because Ripley had heard a lot of ghost stories, but not so many where ghosts were right there. "Also, they said, 'BOO!'"

75

"Perhaps we should have planned for what happened when the ghosts said 'Boo'?" April wondered, making a mental note for her big notebook of scout things.

It is not an easy thing when a mission does not go as planned, a reality that slowly sank in as Roanoke got closer to their cabin.

April sighed. "We should have asked them something!"

"Like what's it like to be a GHOST!" Ripley said. "And can ghosts fly?"

"Also, why Mal's socks," Jo added, bringing them back to their original mission. "Which I believe is why we went there in the first place."

"At least I got some of my socks back," Mal said, pulling a pair out of her pocket.

Molly was quiet. She climbed into her bunk and twisted down under her covers.

It is possible for a person to be terribly frightened and then terribly sleepy. And that's what Roanoke suddenly was. Jen didn't even need to tell them to go to bed when she got to the cabin and turned off the light a few minutes later.

By midnight, everyone was sound asleep. Except for . . . Mal and Molly.

"Hey," Mal whispered. "Are you okay? You're all quiet again."

"Again?" Molly sat up in her bunk. "I'm okay, I'm just thinking."

"About what?"

Molly pulled the snoring Bubbles up onto her lap. "I was just thinking. Like. Why would a ghost go to so much trouble to get us to come to its cabin and then scare us away? It doesn't make sense."

"Maybe the mystery's not solved yet," Mal said.

"Maybe." Molly yawned, sinking into her sleeping bag. "Maybe we can solve it tomorrow."

"Sure," Mal said. "Molly?"

Either Molly or Bubbles or both were snoring. A soft buzz like a bumblebee out for a midnight stroll.

Mal lay on her back.

She had a feeling, like a flutter in her stomach.

A flutter that followed her into her dream, a dream about a lake.

It was the lake near her grandma's cottage. The lake with the white boat and the mysterious ripples on the surface. In her dream, she and Molly were standing on her grandma's dock, playing drums.

Which is weird, because Molly didn't play drums.

But it was a dream.

Mal looked down at her drum and noticed it was soft

and plushy, like moss, instead of hard and easy to hit, like a real drum.

Just then, Mal looked up and saw that Molly was gone.

"Molly?" Dream Mal called out. "MOLLY?"

"MOLLY!"

In the dream, it was like Mal was being squeezed so hard, she couldn't breathe.

"MAL!" Awake-world Molly grabbed Mal by the shoulder. "Wake up!"

Mal rubbed her eyes. "What time is it?"

"Morning," Molly said. "Look."

It was the mirror next to Mal and Molly's bunk. In the light sprinkling of dust on the glass, someone had written in careful print:

Sorry. Please come back. ~D

PART TWO

EVERYTHING'S PARANORMAL

THE GHOST FILES

While the study of science, including biology, chemistry, and physics, is an important part of understanding the world around you, scouts may also pursue the study of those phenomena that fall outside standard areas of study.

Lumberjanes embrace the nontraditional, that which defies traditional explanations. This badge nurtures the interests of scouts that go outside of the known and expected.

To venture into the realm of the unexplained is to consider the possibility of explanations beyond those we expect, which is to consider those expectations and where they come from.

Ghosts, things that go bump in the night, things that play the clarinet in the night, the strange and the surreal are all welcome areas of study for Lumberjanes willing to venture into . . .

CHAPTER 15

In total, there are five known ghosts at Miss Qiunzella Thiskwin Penniquiqul Thistle Crumpet's Camp for Hardcore Lady-Types.

The very first Lumberghost was a kitchen ghost named Inez, who apparated into the kitchen on the very first night of camp and began an aggressive campaign for vegetarian cooking practices.

If Inez had a ghost personal ad it would read:

Inez. Loves vegetables and doing weird scary things. Looking for someone to leave me a gluten-free vegan treat at a disclosed location every night. Must love ghosts.

The night after they first made their presence known, the camp's other four ghosts hovered in front of Roanoke.

Seemingly relatively unsure of what to say.

The moon was bright and shone through the cracks in the well-worn roof of Lake Specter's Ghost Cabin. Mal, Molly, Jo, April, and Ripley all held their flashlights with steady hands and tried not to look freaked out by the fact that they were being addressed by scouts who were no longer alive.

Talking to someone who is dead is very different than talking to a griffin or a unicorn, because most of the griffins and unicorns you talk to are . . . alive.

The ghosts of the Ghost Cabin shifted, their skirts wafting in the nonexistent wind. They tucked their hands in their hazy pockets and pulled bits of hair back behind their ears. They exchanged looks of confusion.

The main goal for any Lumberjane meeting a new person or creature, or entity, or magical thing (the list goes on) is to try to be open and curious, welcoming, and the best Lumberjane possible.

Sometimes it is hard to manage this when the new creature in question is breathing fire on you. But, mostly, this does not happen.

April, in addition to being her Lumberbest, was taking notes.

Jo was mentally calculating what kind of energy would create this sort of phantasmal apparition.

Ripley was holding Bubbles, who was growling a little bit.

Mal was holding Molly's hand, ready to yank her to
safety at a moment's notice.

Molly guessed that the ghosts hovering in the cabin
looked to be about fourteen years old, although it was
hard to tell. They didn't look aged, or wrinkled, or
pruney. They looked almost like holograms of regular
scouts. They looked like what Molly remembered chalk
looking like on the chalkboard after you rubbed off a line
with your palm.

Mal thought their eyes were all slightly darker and more
deep-set than a living person's. The ghosts were all wearing
what looked like very old-fashioned clothes, although their
clothes didn't look old, just long and sort of . . . itchy. Long
wool skirts and thick long-sleeved, button-down shirts,
with stiff kerchiefs tied at their necks.

Molly noted that if you looked at them for a long time,
their edges blurred, like when you try and take a photo of
someone moving. If you looked at them very carefully, you
could see . . . through them.

Although, that is sort of a rude thing to do to a ghost.

Molly blinked.

The ghost scouts exchanged more looks, their hair wisps
floating around their faces like smoke.

Roanoke held their breath and waited. What would be the ghosts' first words? What would be their wisdom from beyond the grave?

Mal looked at Molly and mouthed, "What should we do?"

Finally, one of the ghosts, the shortest ghost, stepped forward and spread her arms wide. She had very very curly hair squashed down by a slightly oversize leather hat.

"Evening, breathbags," she growled in a voice that filled the cabin. "Welcome to Daedalus."

CHAPTER 16

Did you know ghosts sometimes think of living people as very noisy, easily frightened receptacles of oxygen?

It's not something they often discuss, because, as another ghost would quickly point out, that's incredibly rude.

"GREAT PARSNIPS! MAGGIE!" The tallest ghost dove to the front, pushing the shorter ghost back with an aggressive shove. "Manners!"

"HEY!" the shorter one snapped.

"My sincerest apologies," the tall ghost explained. "Margaret is not used to . . . company. None of us are, but that does NOT excuse that sort of language."

"BEANS!" Maggie growled from behind the other ghosts.

The tall ghost cleared her throat, a leftover habit from her own time as a breathbag . . . er, living scout. Speaking in what seemed to Molly and April to be a bit of a British accent, she continued. "Thank you for coming. Of course, we must apologize for the 'Boo' earlier. It was, upon reflection, quite uncalled for."

"I thought it was funny," Maggie the ghost piped in. "Bunch of sprouts. Sent you RUNNING!"

"Ahem," the tall ghost clipped, with a frown. "It was *rude* and we *apologize*."

"Sorry," Maggie deadpanned. "I mean, if we had KNOWN you were coming—"

"Boo-ing," the tall ghost interrupted, "is a ghost maneuver only called for in very specific situations."

April wondered what those would be. She could think of six.

Wait.

Seven.

"Apology accepted," Mal said.

"We are," the ghost continued, "as Maggie has said, the scouts of Daedalus cabin. And, of course, we welcome you."

Roanoke all nodded appreciatively. "Thanks!"

"I am Deborah Anne Delores Fellow," the tall ghost continued.

"I am Margaret Rosaline Caroline Li, but you can call me *Maggie*." The growly, curly-haired scout raised her hand and shook it like a rag doll. "Do NOT call me Margaret."

"My name is Heddie Eleanor Rebecca Ross." The ghost with the braids waved. "Hello."

"I'm Claudia Elizabeth Grace Kelly." A ghost scout with a pair of thin wire spectacles slipped forward.

There was a pause.

"And you are?" Deborah asked, holding out her hand.

"OH! Um. I'll do this." Molly stepped forward. "I'm Molly. This is April, Jo, Mal, and Ripley. And that's Bubbles. We're Roanoke cabin. And we're really happy to meet you."

Roanoke waved, eyes wide. "Hey," they all said in unison, with a smile.

"I hope we're not intruding," Molly continued. "We were under the impression that you wanted us here."

"Yes. We should confess, Claudia is the one who has been *borrowing* your socks," Deborah noted.

"We thought she was just COLLECTING them," Heddie added. "We didn't know they were STOLEN."

Deborah looked at Claudia with what for even a ghost must have qualified as a deadly glare. "Perhaps you could explain, Claudia, your reasoning for this very un-Lumberghost behavior."

"Of course." Claudia nodded, pushing her hair out of her eyes that glowed slightly green. "My reasoning was . . . Yes. You see, we have been scouts here, Lumberghosts, for—"

"Guess how long!" Maggie cut in from behind Deborah.

"A hundred years?" April guessed.

"MASHED POTATOES!!" Maggie scoffed. "A HUNDRED YEARS? What kind of corn-brained—"

"MAGGIE!" Deborah shot Maggie another look. "Great gourds! Perhaps you could be a little more Lumberghost and a little less GHOUL?!"

"It's been a long time," Claudia broke in. "But beyond that, the reason I brought you here is . . ."

Everyone, ghosts included, leaned in to hear Claudia's explanation.

April turned and whispered at a level only Jo could hear. "Please ask us to take part in the first annual ghost games please ask us to take part in the first annual ghost games please ask us to take part in the first annual ghost games please ask us to take part in the first annual ghost games."

"Badges," Claudia finished. "I, or, WE, would like you to help us acquire badges."

"Badges," Deborah coughed.

"Badges," Maggie sputtered.

"Yes." Claudia turned to her fellow ghost scouts and raised her hands in a small celebratory gesture. "Surprise!"

April threw her head back. "GREAT NALO HOPKINSON! THAT IS SO MUCH BETTER THAN GHOST GAMES!"

"Interesting," Jo said. By which she meant, interesting that Claudia's plan meant acquiring badges, and also, interesting that this was news to her fellow scouts.

April jogged from foot to foot with giddy excitement. "You mean you want us to help you get amazing super-cool badges! Badges for LUMBERGHOSTS?!"

Claudia looked around. "I'm sorry, I'm not clear, are you angered by this request?"

Mal shook her head. "No, that's just April's way of telling you, 'Yes, of course we will help you get badges.'"

"WOOT WOOT!" April waved her arms in the air, almost knocking over Ripley. "It's OPERATION GHOST BADGES POSSIBLY TO BE FOLLOWED BY THE FIRST ANNUAL GHOST GAMES WHICH I WILL HELP ORGANIZE AND WILL INVOLVE A GHOST CUP AS A PRIIIIIZE!"

CHAPTER 17

There are many things that people compare to riding a bicycle, sometimes by saying, "It's like riding a bicycle."

Technically, the only thing that's even sort of like riding a bicycle is riding a unicycle. But, as April, who had recently acquired her One Wheel or Another badge, could tell you, riding a one-wheeled bike is not really like riding a bike in that it is MUCH HARDER.

Mostly when people say, "It's like riding a bicycle," they mean that once you learn something, that knowledge will stay with you for a very long time.

This is not necessarily true for ghosts.

This is partly because ghosts, at least some ghosts, have been ghosts for a very very VERY long time. Some for decades or even centuries. And remembering things over that many years can be a little tricky.

If you don't believe me, YOU try it.

In fact, many ghosts, over the years and years they are ghosts, forget a lot of things. One of them being, in this case, how to be a scout.

"As much as I disagree with Claudia's methods," Deborah said, sneaking a sideways glance at Claudia, "it is true, we have possibly lost our way when it comes to our scout duties over the last few decades."

"The whole reason we became Lumberghosts is because we love being scouts," Heddie added. "You know, otherwise we would just be regular ghosts."

"And how would that come about?" Jo asked in a quiet but clear voice.

"The point is," Deborah said, skipping lightly over Jo's question, "we *could* learn a lot from you."

"You breathbags do seem to be getting a lot done, even at night, which is when we do most of our watching you," Maggie said, waggling her ghostly eyebrows.

"Just a quick note." Jo held up a finger. "Generally, we don't accept the practice of calling people derogatory names."

Maggie tilted her head. "I beg your pardon?"

"She's asking you to not call us breathbags." Molly pointed at her chest.

"I'm sure we can avoid calling people names." Deborah nodded, jabbing the smoky edge of Maggie's phantom shoulder with a pointy ghost finger.

"Right right." Maggie nodded with such vigorousness a person identifying as someone living might be worried about losing their head. "Apologies."

"No harm done," Mal said with a wave.

"Is there anything you all like to be called?" Molly added.

"Ghosts is fine," Claudia said, peeking her head forward. "And you?"

"Scouts is fine," Jo said. "Also Lumberjanes. Or . . . people. People is also fine."

"As ghosts," Mal asked, "is there anything we need to consider when it comes to badge getting?"

"There are some restrictions," Deborah noted, floating closer. "We are not generally able to move things heavier than a light utensil."

"Or sock," April noted.

"We also cannot manifest during the day, so whatever we do needs to be done at night," Heddie added.

The members of Roanoke considered.

"So, no solar panels," Jo said.

"No weight lifting," April mused. "Arts and crafts are a

definite possibility, though. Hey! We should probably ask, what kind of badges do you all want to get?"

Heddie raised her hand. "Are there any new badges for budding or lapsed mechanically minded scouts?"

Jo smiled. "There are MANY."

"I wouldn't mind brushing up on my ballroom skills," Maggie said.

"That is a great idea!" Ripley grinned. "Also! Do you like Jazzercise?"

"I have no notion of what that would be," Maggie said.

"You'll see. It's amazing," Ripley said with a solemn nod.

"Goodness," Deborah sighed. "Back when I was a scout, I had so many interests, I really don't know where to start . . ."

"I think we can do something about that!" April charged toward Deborah and threw her arm over Deborah's shoulders in a gesture meant to be reassuring. Of course, ghosts don't have regular shoulders, and April's arm slid through the manifestation of Deborah like it was gliding through a puff of smoke. April put her hands over her mouth. "Oh my gosh, I'm so sorry!"

"It is a ghost thing," Heddie said. "No bodies."

"But NOT nobodies," April said, thrusting her finger in the air. "SCOUTS!"

"YES!" Molly said.

"Absolutely," Mal added.

"And we are here to help you guys be the best ghost scouts you can be," April said, slamming her fist in her palm.

And with that, Operation: Ghost Badges was in effect.

An operation that had a few twists and turns to come.

CHAPTER 18

Here is a quick 101 for those who have not read *In the Spirit* by Miss Jane Petunia Massy Acorn Dale, anthropologist, amateur paranormal researcher, taco enthusiast.

Obviously, there are many kinds of ghosts the same way there are many kinds of people. There are phantoms and spirits (water and land), there are house ghosts and hotel ghosts. Living room and dining room ghosts. Short and tall ghosts. Young and old ghosts.

Some ghosts are very private and some are very public. Some haunt houses, some apartments and condos, some parks and playgrounds.

A curious quality of most ghosts is that they tend to get a bit stuck in their living time. Sort of like how adults are most fond of the music that was popular when they were teenagers, even if that music is "soft rock."

In some ways, Miss Qiunzella's was the perfect place for a ghost, because VERY little of Miss Qiunzella's had changed in terms of the physical camp since Deborah and the rest of Daedalus had been scouts.

There was, for example, very little modern technology allowed at Miss Qiunzella's: no cell phones or computers. There was a radio in Rosie's office, but she only used it to play her favorite radio station, Indigo Magic K45 FM, the only station whose waves could reach through the thick woods surrounding the cabins.

The exception to this rule was Jo's workshop, which was really the Lumberjane mechanical shop, but was inhabited most of the time by Jo.

Outside, the shop looked like a regular warehouse, with a giant metal door secured with a lock that required the first fifteen digits of pi for entry.

Inside, even for modern-day scouts, it was a little like stepping into a science fiction movie. The east wall was covered with shelves on shelves of various parts and tools, all organized by size and use.

On one shelf alone there were: carriage bolts (not necessarily for carriages), lag bolts, flange bolts, eye bolts, U-bolts (curiously, no Me-Bolts). Pretty much any bolt you could think of, and a few Jo was still identifying. There was wood shop equipment on the west side, welding on the east. Over in the northeast corner hummed all the camp's digital technology, next to shelves with basic wiring and circuitry parts, which took up the center islands.

As Heddie floated through the door, Jo flipped on a switch and the shop hummed to life. It was like a well-oiled machine, full of well-oiled machines. It even had its own melody of noises: clicks and whirs from the various electrical devices.

"This is HUGE." Heddie spun around.

The shop was impressive and one-fifth the size of Jo's shop at home.

"It's pretty impressive," Jo said.

"Great gourds, this is . . ." Heddie's hand fluttered to her lips. "This is . . . Is . . ."

"Yeah, I know, right?" Jo knew that sometimes there were no words to express how cool something was. "Sometimes in my sleep I reorganize it."

"Well, I think you have done a remarkable job." Heddie stood in front of the shelves, arms out. "It is wonderful, Jo."

"Thanks!" Jo held out her arms. "Take a look around!"

Against the fluorescent light of the shop, Heddie's outline was fainter, but it was easy to see she was dazzled. She swooped over the truck engine Jo was refitting for biodiesel use, floated over a set of solar panels Jo was repairing and a set of circuit boards she was tinkering with for reasons that weren't yet clear.

At one point, Heddie literally dove into an engine, like a kid diving into a swimming pool.

Jo blinked. "Now, that would be a useful trick."

"It IS extraordinary what you can do when you don't have a living body to carry around," Heddie said, completely hidden inside the engine. "I wonder if it would have helped my father, to be able to do something like this."

"What did your father do?" Jo asked.

"He was a fireman. Worked for the railway." Heddie's eyes appeared.

"Oh, for trains! That's awesome." Jo raised an eyebrow. "My dads build rockets."

"Your *dads*?" Heddie asked, her voice echoing. "You have two?"

"I do." Jo nodded, stepping over to a light plastic drone she was fitting with a new set of propellers.

"That's a lot of . . . dad," Heddie remarked, her face now peeking up out of the engine.

"Sometimes it's just enough dad," Jo noted. "Sometimes, it's a lot of dad. But it's definitely cool getting to talk about science all the time. Which is pretty much all we do at home."

"That sounds heavenly." Heddie's full head bobbed up from inside the engine. She looked like she was at a Halloween party dressed up as the inside of a truck.

Jo considered. "So, if you don't mind me asking, what's it like being in Daedalus? You know, being with the same scouts for so long? What do you all talk about?"

Heddie pulled herself out of the engine. "Oh, you know, the things Lumberghosts talk about. Over and over again." Heddie threw her hands up. "Every. Night."

"Is everything . . . okay?" Jo asked, spinning the drone's propeller slowly with her finger.

Heddie drifted toward Jo and into the table with the hovercraft, her middle half disappearing and reappearing. "Honestly, if it is all the same to you, Jo, I would love to just talk about . . . whatever it is you think about when you are in the process of building something."

Jo set the drone down on a table. "You mean talk *shop*? We can definitely do that."

"Thanks." Heddie seemed to relax slightly. "Just . . . for a little reprieve."

Jo walked over to a table of metal wrenches and pliers. "What do you want to build? What did you build when you were a scout? Or, you know, alive?"

"Lots of things. Mostly with wood." Heddie looked closely at Jo's table of screws and hammers.

"We could make a boxcar," Jo said, making space on her bench. "That would probably work toward you getting your Make It Torque badge."

Heddie looked up.

"You know," Jo offered, "where torque is . . ."

"A force that causes rotation! Yes, of course!" Heddie looked down at her ghost hands. "There's just, the small problem of . . . I'm not very good at picking up things in the living world. That's more Maggie and Claudia's specialty."

Maggie was currently learning to pop and lock for her It's Poppin' badge with Ripley. She was very good at popping, but less good at locking.

Jo held up a finger as she dug into her pockets. "I think I have just the thing."

Jo pulled from her pocket the small silver screwdriver her dads had mailed her, still shiny and unscathed. "This is pretty light," she said with a grin, placing the tool on the bench.

Heddie smiled. "Thank you, Jo. I am really so glad, you know, that we are doing this. I hope . . . I hope it helps. Everyone, I mean. Daedalus."

Jo rolled her eyes. "I feel very confident that the Lumberghosts of Daedalus will soon be earning what my very good friend April would want to describe as BUCKETS of badges."

Heddie looked at Jo. "You are good scouts. I could tell right away."

"Well, we do our best," Jo said.

105

"Indeed," Heddie said. Twisting her nose in concentration, she reached her hand toward the screwdriver, palm up, fingers beckoning. She touched her fingertip to the edge of the screwdriver, held her breath, as much as any ghost can, and focused every bit of phantasmal energy into the tip of her index finger. There was a squeaking sound, a scritchy-scratchy sound, and, just like that, the edge of the handle swiveled slightly and slid into Heddie's hand.

"Great gobs of garlic," Heddie cheered. "Success!"

There was something bothering Jo. She couldn't quite put her finger on it.

It was something about Daedalus, about Claudia's plan to bring the scouts to the cabin to get badges. It was bugging her, like a slightly loose screw that gave off a little shake, a persistent rattle.

Heddie twirled the screwdriver on her finger. "Think I might get a handle on this!"

"Heddie," Jo began. "Is there something . . ."

Heddie looked up, her face triumphant. "Yes?"

Jo remembered that Heddie had waited a very long time to talk shop. She buttoned her lip.

"Yes, Jo?" Heddie repeated.

Jo grabbed her favorite drafting pencil. "Never mind. Let's get to work!"

CHAPTER 19

Mal was trying not to look at Claudia, but it is hard not to look at something you have never seen before, especially when that something, a ghost, is something you've been told probably doesn't exist.

Not that seeing things that don't exist was all that rare an experience for any of the members of Roanoke cabin, who had seen a good many things a regular, not-Lumberjane scout might not expect to see.

This would include: a gargoyle, a griffin (actually, several griffins), a unicorn, and snow in summer.

(Pagophobia is a fear of ice or frost. There is no specific phobia name for snow in summer. Although, it is weird.)

Still. Watching a being hovering a few inches off the ground, who was there and not there, whose eyes were both eyes and also gray windows to another world, was kind of . . . cool.

Molly noticed that it looked like some sort of breeze was always wafting around Claudia, ruffling the fabric of her skirt and teasing stray hairs loose from her braid. This same inexplicable breeze also made the hairs on Molly's arms stand up.

Molly bit her lip. Staring is rude. How long had they all just been standing and staring?

"So," she said, looking at Mal with wide eyes. "SO. Mal."

"So! Yes! Claudia." Mal started to attention, and Claudia spun around to face them.

"Yes!" Claudia clutched her hand to her chest. "So. Yes. We should get started! With the badges? Yes? The badge? Or is it a pin?"

Back in the cabin, Claudia had had plenty of ideas for the other Daedalus scouts, and paired each of them up—Heddie with Jo, Maggie with Ripley, April with Deborah. But then, once everyone had filed out to work on their badges, Claudia seemed to be a bit . . . lost when it came to her own plans. Like, when it came to her OWN interests, she didn't have a plan.

Finally, it was Mal who came up with the idea of the Library pin, which required scouts to research five subjects using the resources available in the local library.

Now that they were in the library, Claudia seemed . . . distracted.

Flustered, Mal thought, or just like she had something on the stove, or like she was waiting for someone to walk through the door.

"Was the library here when you were a scout?" Molly asked, imagining that Claudia was just intimidated. "The ship?"

"Oh, yes. It was here, but it wasn't a library, it was just a ship. A red ship," Claudia said. "Red like a rose. I think it was even called *The Rose*."

Claudia drifted through the stacks of books, actually through them. "It's funny. It's hard to remember when it became a library. One of those ghost things I suppose, stuff appearing and disappearing."

Inside the library, lamps burned with a soft glow, making the ship feel like a warm, cozy cave . . . of knowledge. Everything inside the ship was quiet, so every squeak, even a beetle scurrying across the floor, sounded like a parade.

Also, Molly sniffed, it smelled like beeswax.

"So. To get your Book and See Library pin," Mal said, running a finger over the spines of Lumberjane handbooks, "you need to read at least five books on five different sub-jects, ideally in at least two different genres."

Variety is the spice of life, as Lumberjanes and avid readers know.

"So," Molly continued, stepping toward the shelves, "your subjects could be anything, really. Like: cooking, oh, maybe not cooking, um, astronomy or textiles or . . . ?"

Claudia looked at them expectantly. "What did you do?"

"Greek mythology, astronomy, and archery," Molly said. "And then I read a book on raccoons and some books on the history of the accordion." Molly blushed, shoving her hands into her pockets. "I mean, you know, it's not the most adventurous but . . ."

"I thought you had an amazing selection," Mal cut in. "Claudia, did you know that Molly practically speaks rac-coon now?"

Molly rolled her eyes. "Yeah, right. I'm super talented."

"Hey." Mal furrowed her brows. "You ARE."

"Why don't I read Molly's books?" Claudia clapped her hands, a gesture that made curiously little sound.

Molly looked at Mal. "You can," she said slowly, "but you should do something that interests YOU. Like, what are you interested in?"

"OH, um." Claudia sighed, looking up at the endless stacks. "I don't know."

"Okay, how about this? If you had one thing that you could know more about . . ." Mal held up her hands. "Like RIGHT now, what would it be?"

Claudia floated over a candle, which had the effect of illuminating her entire shape, so it briefly looked like she was on fire, or lit up like a ghost lantern, an effect Claudia didn't seem to notice, but which was sort of blowing Mal's and Molly's minds.

"Is there . . ." Claudia paused, looking down, her hair drifting over her eyes. "A book about . . . cities?"

"Of course!" Molly pulled a book off the shelf, *Building on What We Know*. "Oh! You mean like how to BUILD a city?"

"Or! Any particular cities?" Mal scanned the shelves. "Chicago? New Orleans? Paris? London? New York, maybe?"

"New York." Claudia drifted over to where Mal was standing. "Is there a book on New York?"

"Oh, um, I'm sure there is." Molly's shoulders dropped. "I mean, I know it's super cool there, so there's probably something."

Molly disappeared into the shelves and returned after a few minutes of quiet searching with a large black book.

"Hey," Mal whispered, noticing the sudden drop in Molly's smile, "okay?"

"Sure," Molly said, opening the book on the table for Claudia. It was about New York's bridges. In it, a picture from the early 1900s showed the Brooklyn Bridge, a great arch with lines of metal, like giant spiderwebs. A man in a top hat held a little girl's hand as they walked toward the camera.

"Oh," Mal said, skimming the page with her finger. "It's like the history of New York."

"Sorry," Molly said in a sad voice.

Mal put a reassuring hand on Molly's shoulder. "This is fine! It's awesome!"

Claudia put her face so close to the book her chin disappeared into the pages. "So this is what it looks like now?"

Mal flipped the page. "I mean, the bridge is still there, but the city is KERNUTS. It's, like, all neon and big giant buildings and billboards and stuff. It's awesome."

"I would like to see a book on that," Claudia said quietly. "On what New York looks like . . . now. If that is all right."

"Of course," Molly said. "But . . ."

Outside, the wisps of dawn were creeping in the doorway. "Maybe we can read it tomorrow night!"

"That would be very nice," Claudia said. "You're both . . . very nice . . . friends?"

Molly smiled. "Sure! Friends. I'm so glad we could help you, Claudia."

Claudia looked over to the door, to the blush of sun that was creeping in. "I have to go. But, I want to thank you . . . for helping me. And ask you . . ."

Molly yawned. The lack of sleep was starting to vibrate in her bones, making everything suddenly very heavy. "Yes?"

"Please don't tell the other scouts, Daedalus, about this. About my research . . ."

"Because . . ." Mal tilted her head.

"I just. I want it to be a surprise."

"Okay." Mal could feel a frown from Molly without even looking. "Sure. I mean."

"If you want it to be a surprise," Molly said.

Claudia beamed. "Thank you!"

As sunlight flooded the ship, Claudia's smile was the last bit of her to disappear.

CHAPTER 20

The next morning, Ripley, who had literally been dancing all night, was so sound asleep, not even Jen's "WAKE UP, SCOUTS" seemed to wake her.

And Jen's "WAKE UP, SCOUTS" was very loud.

"What were you all up to last night?" Jen marveled, holding a mirror to Ripley's nose to make sure she was still breathing.

"Night dancing," April said. "It's for our new, uh, Night Dancing badge, er, PLAY."

"Dancing Under the Stars," Mal added.

"Hmmmm." Jen checked her watch, then looked up at the smiling scouts of Roanoke with a fair amount of suspicion. "All right, then. I have a canoe trip to supervise, but someone check on her to make sure she doesn't sleep through lunch."

"I'll do it," Molly offered. "I have . . . some reading to do."

After breakfast, Mal, April, and Jo had their Hop, Skip, and a Jump badge to work on, so they joined a dozen trios of scouts on the small paved circle behind the mess hall. Barney, who was on a team with Hes and Wren, waved.

April yawned and waved back. "You know, with ghost scout time and day scout time, it's like we're double scouts."

Jo stifled her own yawn as she untangled their ropes. "Even vampires sleep in the day."

Mal was seeing spots. Also, she could feel each individual ray of sun on every part of her skin. Who knew the sun was so loud?

April leaned up against the tree, stretching her calves in prep. "So what did you do with Claudia?"

"You know, even though the whole thing was her idea, it didn't seem like she really knew what she wanted to do, badge-wise," Mal admitted. "In the end, we worked on her Library pin."

Jo smiled. "Heddie was so into working in the shop. I mean, imagine, you haven't really been an active scout in maybe decades? I'm sure it feels good for them to be busy again."

"Deborah was super into it." April switched calves. "She has like a million badges she wants to do. Which is obviously the perfect number."

Mal shrugged. "I mean, Claudia was . . . appreciative. Maybe it's just overwhelming to suddenly have a bunch of choices."

"Ooh!" April looked up. "That reminds me. I'm a subject away from finishing *my* Library pin!"

"All right, scouts," Vanessa hollered, bouncing in her bright red sneakers, her hair spikes glinting in the sun. "I want to see less chatting, more skipping!"

Jo passed two handles of the ropes to Mal and walked a few feet away. "Does it seem odd to you? Claudia's plan, as a plan? I mean, stealing socks so we could come to Daedalus and help them get badges? Like, if that was her plan, wouldn't she be super excited to get a badge? You know?"

"I don't know . . ." April considered, stepping into the ropes. "Some plans are a little weird."

Some of April's plans had been a little weird. April was completely willing to defend 99 percent of her plans.

"It just seems . . ." Jo paused. "Odd. Not odd. Indirect."

Mal shrugged. "Maybe that's just how ghosts work."

"More turning less talking!" Vanessa hollered.

Jo and Mal, on separate ends of the ropes, started turning them in time.

Aretha Franklin, Doris Day!
G. Willow Wilson, Beyoncé!
Ruth Bader Ginsburg, Coretta Scott King!
Edith Windsor, Carole Pope! SING!

After an hour of double Dutch, Mal, Jo, and April were double flattened and lying out on the grass to catch their breath.

"Idea!" April's arm shot up. "What if I do my last section of my Library pin on Lumberjane history! Then maybe I could find out more about Daedalus!"

"That's a good idea," Jo said, still too tired to move. "We could use some more information. Also, maybe, some calories. Maybe we need chocolate."

"Very good idea," Mal added.

April, whose energy came from some distant magical source, bounced up from the ground. "Don't want to SKIP out on you, but—"

Jo groaned.

"I want to get started," April continued. "Someone check on Ripley?"

"Molly said she would," Jo said.

And with a distinct zipping sound, April was off.

"Speaking of, where is Molly?" Jo asked.

"She said she's reading, but I think she's doing the math homework her mom sent," Mal said, staring at the cloud

that looked a little Molly-shaped. "She doesn't talk about it, but I know that stuff makes her real sad."

Jo nodded, knowing that stuff from home can be an unwelcome interruption to Lumberfun. Not that Jo would call it Lumberfun out loud. "It's one thing to send someone a nice physics equation, it's another to send actual HOMEWORK."

Mal rolled over on the grass so the blades tickled her chin. "Yeah. Yesterday Claudia was asking stuff about New York and I could see it bummed Molly out."

Jo rolled over to look at Mal. "What did Claudia want to know about New York?"

"Oh." Mal grabbed a blade of grass and squished it between her fingers. "I don't know. She asked us not to tell Daedalus, though."

"Really?" Jo sat up. "That's weird."

Mal sat up. "You know what? You're right!"

"I think I am." Jo squinted at a cloud that looked a little like an octahedron.

Mal pushed herself up to a stand. "We need to find something ELSE to do with Claudia so we don't talk about New York. If we can avoid talking about stuff that upsets Molly, she won't be upset, and maybe she can forget the totally uncool package her mom sent."

"Okay," Jo said. Not that that was what Jo was right about.

"Thanks for the talk, Jo!"

Jo watched Mal sprint off into the sunshine.

"Riiiight," she said. Which is another way of saying, "NOT right," as in "Something's not right, something's NOT right at all."

121

CHAPTER 21

A dance floor is a magical space. It's a place where music transforms a person into a dancer.

Dead or (stayin') alive.

This is what Ripley, who was dressed in her very best most sparkly leg warmers and matching headband and jumper, matching Bubbles's leg warmers and headband, believed with all her heart and dancing soul.

"Right." Ripley circled back to the sound system and selected the next track. "So now we're going to work on our power moves."

Admittedly, at first, Ripley hadn't been sure how much Maggie was going to be into dancing. At first Maggie mostly made fun of the music, all of which she thought was "too noisy."

"What the SPROUT! You have to play everything all at once all the time?" she'd grumbled, hovering near the ceiling, like she was trying to stay as far away from the sound as possible.

"This music is BROCCOLI!"

By which Maggie meant "bad."

It was also possible that Maggie didn't like Bubbles, who also didn't like Maggie, as was evident from the low growl Ripley could hear rumbling under the music.

Ripley was undeterred, which is to say, not in any way bummed out by Maggie's somewhat unpositive attitude about the music Ripley picked, because Ripley knew that the key was finding the RIGHT music.

If you don't like ABBA, there's Rihanna, if you don't like Rihanna, there's Sleater-Kinney. Don't like Sleater-Kinney? There's lots of other things to choose from.

Music soothes everybody—savage beasts, grouchy ghosts, the whole lot.

And for Maggie, that music was MISSY ELLIOTT.

As soon as she heard Missy, Maggie floated down. "HOLY TOMATO," she squealed, her curls bouncing. "What is THIS?!"

"It's good," Ripley said, momentarily unsure. "Right?"

"You bet your beans it is!" Maggie closed her eyes and twirled around the room like a plastic bag blowing in a storm.

123

Now, with the right soundtrack, Maggie was a dancing FOOL who was only a few moves away from her Jeté Set Go! badge, having mastered her Tour Jeté, Petit Jeté, and Glissade.

Given that Maggie was not at all affected by gravity, great leaps were kind of her specialty.

Really there was pretty much no move Maggie couldn't do. Except tap. Tap was a bit of a stretch for someone who had trouble making noise with her feet, because her feet didn't really hit the ground.

While Ripley rested, because Ripley didn't have a ghost body and she got tired, Maggie floated like a starfish on her back in the center of the dance floor, three feet in the air, as the disco ball lights shone through her.

"I will say," Maggie spread her fingers out and stretched. "This is divine."

"Yeah! I'm glad we get to dance together," Ripley cheered. "Dancing is the best. I'm sorry you can't wear leg warmers, but it's still the best."

"I am good with what I have on," Maggie said. "Once you've been wearing something for this long, it's sort of a second skin. Thanks, though."

Amazingly Maggie didn't have to worry about keeping her hat on her head, since ghost hats are far more securely fastened than your average living person hat.

Ripley tried to imagine wearing the same thing every day for decades. It wasn't all that difficult. Ripley pretty much wore the same thing every day already.

"You know," Maggie sighed, "as much as she is a pain in the potato, that Claudia did a good turn bringing you all to Daedalus."

"I think so, too," Ripley said, adjusting her headband. "Wait. Where's the potato?"

"Deborah would say it's impolite to say, but . . ." Maggie twisted a ghostly curl around her finger. "Of course, Claudia and Heddie and Deborah are my best friends in the whole world. And Claudia will always be my scout sister, even when she is a bit of a pinch in the greens."

Ripley was still not sure where the greens were, but it didn't seem worth pushing.

Maggie twisted onto her side. "Should we get back to dancing?"

"I think we should," Ripley said, hands on hips. "I hope your potato ends up okay."

"I have little doubt that it will sort itself out," Maggie said, stretching out her arms. "When you have an eternity, you don't have much choice."

CHAPTER 22

There is no specific time that night begins or ends. For some people, night is when you go to bed, for some people it's when it's no longer light. It starts roughly when the sun is no longer in the sky, when reading outside is hard without a flashlight, and ends when it feels like it's time for breakfast.

In this way, night is subjective, which means it's night when you define it as night. Within reason. Noon, on any given day, is hardly night.

For ghosts, night is something that happens, a pull to a state of being. For ghosts, night is a very personal thing and day is a mystery, always out of reach.

But, as April learned, this was something that never bothered Deborah, who had always been what she called "fair" and so hated the sun, which tended to leave her with a bright red burn. Deborah loved everything about the night, including the various creatures that called the night-time their hour.

Ghosts are natural bird-watchers, partly because they are also the best tree climbers. Not that ghosts actually have to climb trees. Instead, Deborah glided up the tree they'd chosen as April huffed her way up a branch, so they could observe the movements of barn owls, who seemed to be out for some sort of barn owl gathering that evening.

At the top branch, where April and Deborah settled, a chill evening breeze rippled through the needles with a satisfying swishing noise. The chill made April pull her sweater around herself, noting that, obviously, ghosts don't really care about the cold.

Deborah floated over the branch a few inches away from April, her skirt billowing around her legs with boots that disappeared in the shafts of moonlight that filtered through the trees.

April had to remind herself that Deborah, as a ghost, didn't have to keep a hand on the branch above her. Also that April DID.

In addition to owl watching, April was taking advantage of Deborah's knowledge to add to her research on the history of the Lumberjanes. Obviously the best resource is the person who was actually THERE when the history was happening. Also, there were suprisingly not a lot of books on the history of the Lumberjanes in the library. Fortunately, Deborah seemed pleased to be a resource, so much so that she quickly forgot the owls and seemed to lose herself in memory.

"In some ways camp was the same," Deborah said, "in some ways very different. In my day, we didn't have cabins, we had tents. And you could look down from the hill and see all of us set up in perfect rows all lined up with their perfect peaks of canvas . . ."

April shivered. "Cabins are cozier."

"Tents *are* a bit chilly." Deborah nodded. "And damp in the rain and hot in the sun. But I was never bothered. To me, it was an adventure. My young life at home was comfortable, I was fortunate, but it was also truly tedious. The most interesting years of my life were those I spent as a Lumberjane." Deborah looked up at the stars. "To be a scout, I would have slept on a rock."

"Me too." April hoped that there was not a badge she would eventually have to get that meant sleeping on a rock. "I mean, yeah, hopefully we won't have to, but yeah, I would."

April would later try sleeping on a rock just to see if it was possible. It is, but it is kind of a miserable night.

April paused. "Was it hard to maneuver in your . . . uniform?"

"In a long wool skirt? Yes." Deborah kicked her ghost feet, causing her skirt to puff up like a fluffy cloud. "My counselor insisted that a scout should be able to run in whatever they're given to run in, as fast as they need to run. When duty called, I was ready and able. Always."

"Hardcore." April kicked her non-ghost feet. "Would have been nice to have pants, though, right?"

"I do like your britches." Deborah smiled. "Are they wool?"

"Polyblend. I basically have one pair of shorts," April admitted. "Being a Lumberjane when you were a scout sounds like it was a lot of work."

"Being a person when I was a living person was a lot of work. Being a Lumberjane was and is an honor. I cannot imagine a better place to spend the afterlife than here. Even with its restrictions, being a part of Daedalus is our . . . destiny."

"Can I ask . . ." April looked down at the ground far below and hoped her next question was not super super rude. "You didn't all . . . die here, did you?"

"Oh goodness, no!" Deborah chuckled.

"Okay, phew." April wiped her brow, careful not to let go with her left hand. "I was hoping there wasn't a terrible Lumbertragedy to go with your camp story."

Deborah shook her head. "No, we all, well, we grew up, April. We grew up and left camp and did other things, many of us inspired by our work as scouts. I was a teacher. It was one of the few jobs a woman could have back then. I found it incredibly rewarding. Of course, I dabbled in other things, like writing and art. But mostly I was a teacher and my husband was a doctor."

There were so many things April wanted to be when she grew up. The list, at the back of one of her many notebooks, was twelve pages long, and alphabetized. "But you missed being a scout?"

"Every day." Deborah sighed.

"Well," April said, perking up, "then it's a good thing you got to come back and be a Lumberghost!"

"It is a choice I will never regret," Deborah said.

In the distance, a barn owl hooted in agreement.

"I was wondering . . ." Deborah held a hand up over her eyes and looked off into the trees, like an actor spotting the cue to her next scene. "I noticed the frame at the entrance of the camp, it used to read MISS QIUNZELLA THISKWIN PEN-NIQUIQUL THISTLE CRUMPET'S CAMP FOR GIRLS."

"Is that what it was?" April said. She'd always wondered what was under that plank on the sign.

"Yes." Deborah looked at April quizzically. "What is a . . . Hardcore Lady-Type?"

"It's people who are . . ." April considered. "It's people who are the most of who they are, who feel like they can be that most . . . here. A LADY-TYPE, that's for anyone who is a lady-type. It's an open invitation to anyone who wants to be awesome."

"Forever and ever," Deborah said, looking up at the moon shining through the trees.

"I have to say," April added, "you're much nicer than the older scout I met at the top of the mountain that was not a mountain, next to a field of smelly unicorns. She was very grouchy and way more worried about ribbons and winning stuff than you are."

"The mountain that's not a mountain." Deborah looked over at April. "You'll have to tell me about that some night."

Talking to Deborah made April's chest buzz with excitement. This was probably, in April's humble opinion, the coolest conversation a scout could have.

Just then a feather caught Deborah's eye. She pointed at the tree next to them, several branches up. "Look!"

The light made her hand glow, April thought, like that line you draw with a sparkler in the air.

CHAPTER 23

That night in the library, while Ripley and Maggie danced, and Deborah and April sought out owls, Mal did her best to change the subject.

While Claudia floated in the candlelight, Mal tap-danced around the stack of books she was hoping Claudia would find infinitely more interesting than the books on New York the librarian had pulled for them that morning.

"You know, I just thought maybe we could do something else," Mal said in a slightly abnormally high pitch, like the voice a salesperson uses to sell perfume no one wants. She picked up some of the other books she'd pulled. "I found a book on Norse mythology, which I thought could be interesting. And this one on card tricks, which, I don't know, don't ghosts like card tricks?"

"Why can't we read about New York?" Molly raised an eyebrow.

"I mean . . ." Mal looked up at the ceiling, like the answer was written there. "You know, New York is FINE, I just don't know how useful . . . it is for a GHOST! Right? Like, Claudia is a ghost *here*, so . . ."

It is difficult to give an answer when you are making up the answer while it's coming out of your mouth. Which Mal was, because why NOT New York? Because Mal was afraid if they talked about New York any more, then Molly would be sad and Molly being sad was like the worst stomach-ache ever.

Claudia looked at the stack of books. Touched it with her translucent fingers. She looked up.

"Because. Because . . . I can never go to New York." Claudia was suddenly as close to Mal as she had ever been. So close Mal could both see her and see through her. "Is that what you're saying? That's why I shouldn't read about it?"

"Oh! No!" Mal leaned back, her stomach dropping. "I'm sorry, I didn't mean to imply that, Claudia."

"She didn't mean . . ." Molly stopped. "She's just. I mean . . . Actually, I'm not sure wha—"

135

Claudia sunk down, like she was melting into the floor. "It's fine."

Obviously it wasn't.

"Wait. Do you . . ." Molly stepped forward. "Do you want to . . . go?"

"To New York?" Mal asked.

"Yes," Claudia said in a bare whisper.

"Okay, well, I mean." Mal looked at Claudia. "Can you?"

Claudia stared at her hands, her eyes sparkling lightning bug green. "Do you know how long I've been here?"

Mal looked at Molly. Maybe they should have asked. "No, we don't."

"I've been here for longer than I can even remember now," Claudia said, drifting up. "I've been here for so many summers and winters. For so long I don't even know how to put it into words. I've been here . . . forever."

There was something in Claudia's voice, Molly thought, like a reed, a trembling of such sadness.

"I made a choice," Claudia said. "WE did, a long long time ago. A choice I didn't understand. A choice I couldn't have understood then. But now, now I am trapped in that choice for eternity.

"Mal, Molly." Claudia pulled on her braid. "I came to you because I need your help."

"How can we help?" Molly asked.

Claudia dropped down so she was eye level with Mal and Molly, standing in between them like a bridge. "Only you can help me leave. And they're not going to want you to. But you have to, Mal, Molly, you have to.

"Please."

CHAPTER 24

O f all the things a person can be afraid of, the dark is right up there with the most common.

Fear of the dark, or nyctophobia, is actually not so much a fear of the dark itself, but of what hides inside the dark.

It's a fear of what you cannot see, when what you cannot see is everything because it is dark.

Scouts at Miss Qiunzella's, especially if they're from a city, often need time to adjust to just how very very dark it gets in the country at night. Without streetlights, the dark in the cabin at night is what's called pitch-black.

You can hold your hand up to your face and not see it.

Sometimes, lying in bed at night, the dark reminded Mal of the lake near her grandma's cottage, which always seemed black to Mal. Deep and mysterious, a place where anything could disappear: flip-flops, toys, maybe even people.

Mal lay on her bunk, her invisible hand inches from her face, the sounds of sleep all around.

"Molly," Mal whispered. "Are you awake?"

"Yes," Molly whispered back.

"What do you think," Mal said in a hushed voice, "about what Claudia said? About helping her leave?"

It was impossible to see the face Molly was making. The face attached to the whisper.

Mal leaned out of her bunk, stared intently up into the dark, opened her eyes as wide as she could, and tried to see past the thick blanket of night. "Molly?"

Molly was silent. So silent, Mal wondered if she'd fallen back asleep.

Claudia had said the only way she could leave was with Roanoke's help. She didn't say what that would be. But probably, given the combined powers of April, Jo, Ripley, Mal, and Molly, they could figure it out. It was kind of what they did. Which would normally make Mal feel pretty chuffed. But in the dark of night, waiting for Molly to answer, it made her insides feel cold, like little snowflakes floating around in her stomach.

"We could ask April and Jo and Ripley," Mal whispered so softly it was barely a sound.

"Yeah," Molly whispered back. "Good night, Mal."

"Good night, Molly," Mal said, turning over to face the wall, not that she could see it. Mal drifted into a strange sleep about lakes and rivers.

CHAPTER 25

April lay flat on her back, next to her pile of books, baking in the sun.

(Fear of sunlight is heliophobia, experienced by vampires, ghosts, and scouts who just really don't like the sun.)

"Holy Afua Richardson." She squinted, her cheeks burning. "It's like I AM the sun. It's like a ball of fire!"

Jo, who was also taking a moment of lying-down time, shielded her eyes. "I feel like we are in definite need of some vitamin D."

"Good thing Jen was out on a hike last night." Ripley dug her toes into the grass. "Or we'd have to explain how we're living like bat people."

"Do you think ghosts miss sunshine?" Ripley asked, holding up a hand and preparing to execute her first of a hundred cartwheels of the day. "If I were a ghost, I would miss sunshine."

"Speaking of missing." Jo lifted her head. "Where are Mal and Molly?"

"I think they're going to Barney's next presentation on water safety," April replied. "'Even More Water Safety.'"

"Okay, well." Jo wiped the blades of grass off her palms. "I'm off to work on my and Heddie's latest. We're upgrading the scuba suit! If anyone is interested in perfecting a sub pump, that's where I'll be."

"I'm cartwheeling," Ripley said, wheeling off down the hill. "Later!"

"I'm reading," April said, grabbing a book from the top of her stack, a thin and very old-looking book covered in red leather.

"Okay." Jo waved.

After her search for books on the history of the Lumberjanes yielded few results, April turned to books written BY Lumberjanes, of which there were many, including the book April held in her hand. It was so old, the leather was soft like a baby blanket. The gold lettering was faded, and April had to tilt the cover toward the sun to read the faded gilt.

The Pact

By D. Morrow.

"Who is D. Morrow?" April wondered out loud.

She opened the front page of the book, and read the dedication.

To My Fellow Scouts, My Lumbersisters

Maggie, Heddie, and Claudia

"Holy Cherie Dimaline," April gasped. "D. Morrow is Deborah!"

CHAPTER 26

Deborah Morrow could not explain exactly why it was that one day she put pen to paper and wrote the book that would eventually be titled *The Pact*. A book that would later be acquired by the honorable Miss Beatrice Frances Margaret Halpern Hottentotenside II, then camp director of Miss Qiunzella Thiskwin Penniquiqul Thistle Crumpet's. Miss Hottentotenside tucked it away in the shelves of her private study, next to a collection of objects guarded by all camp directors, in a room that Rosie currently uses for her moose tack and kombucha.

Deborah Morrow wrote *The Pact* on the day of her thirtieth birthday, after eating strawberry shortcake with her husband. She wrote it because she was afraid she would forget the details of the events described and think it was all a dream. Because that was already happening to some of her memories of being a scout. Memories of roaring rivers and mountain faces. Memories of running wild through the night with her best friends. All had taken on a faded quality she found unnerving.

But that's what happens to memories sometimes.

Miss Hottentotenside read *The Pact* on the day of her thirty-fifth birthday, which fell in the middle of summer, after eating a birthday vegan flan, which Hottentotenside found quite enjoyable. She wondered if *The Pact* was fantasy as opposed to a description of events that actually took place. She couldn't decide, then she put the book back on her shelf next to a glowing blue stone that reminded her of the ocean.

Miss Rachel Upley Rosen Needleprick, another revered camp director, found *The Pact* behind the shelf when she was cleaning up many years later. It was next to a sock she'd been looking for for quite some time. Noticing that an alumnus wrote it, she read it, enjoyed it greatly, and moved it to the recently established ship-turned-library.

Many scouts, like April, who had moved into the shade and continued to read with voracious interest, picked up *The Pact* when they were trying for their Library pins, and liked it well enough, although several scouts noted it was a little short. As the number of books in the library grew, *The Pact* worked its way to a stack that was less popular with scouts, who all preferred what they thought was more informative reading, and eventually it was shuffled to the bottom of a stack of books in the back of the ship.

The Pact is a very well-written, poetic book, with a judicious approach to metaphor and simile that all the scouts who found it in the library, including April, appreciated.

It describes the adventures of the scouts of Daedalus cabin, four smart and able and dedicated scouts who took scouting so seriously, they took it upon themselves to spend extra time working on their maneuvers, which they were very good at. Also, they pitched a perfect tent and got along better than any other cabin. Although one scout was a little rude and called people names. So much so that she eventually started calling them vegetables, which was still a little odd, but less rude. And then eventually that caught on and the whole cabin started doing it.

Anyway, it was the practice of practicing maneuvers that eventually led them to the Wiggly Woods, which were just as wiggly then as they are now, and to a labyrinth that a very busy witch had built there, to keep a very special object, the Specter's Seal, safe from the prying eyes of the not many people who lived there at the time.

The labyrinth was covered in thick ivy, so thick it eventually curved over the tops of the walls and covered the maze completely, making it like a twisting, confusing tunnel. It took them a while, and a few scouts got grouchy, but eventually they made it to the center of the labyrinth and the Seal.

The Seal was something Deborah had read about many weeks before she laid eyes on it, in a similarly very old book in the library, which was then located in the camp director's study. When Deborah learned that the Specter's Seal was real, she revealed to her fellow scouts what, according to her research, it could do.

The Specter's Seal was rumored to have belonged to more than a dozen powerful and mysterious figures, with names like Pricilla the Powerful, Maybelle the Maleficent, and Jane, Just Jane, over the many centuries of its existence.

It is about the size of a dinner plate, made of a seemingly ordinary rock, like the kind you see on a beach or in a mountain.

The Specter's Seal is a powerful and mysterious object; it holds the power to grant its possessor a single wish.

The then owner of the Seal was an older woman named Beatrice the Benign, who was rumored to be saving her wish for a very specific thing, which involved apples.

Beatrice, at the time, had been certain the Seal was well hidden. But it is very difficult to keep things well hidden from Lumberjanes. Lumberjanes are both very good at figuring out things, and pretty dogged in their pursuits.

Mind you, even with her research, Deborah did not know for sure that the Specter's Seal would be so effective, that it would grant the wish they all agreed on. The wish they all made that day, with their hands gripping the gravelly edge of the stone.

Deborah thought the wish they wished was the perfect wish. In *The Pact*, it is the perfect wish.

But it is hard to say exactly what the perfect wish is.

Notably, the specific wish, as spoken by Deborah on that clear night, was "To be ghosts at Miss Qiunzella Thiskwin Penniquiqul Thistle Crumpet's Camp for Girls."

A wish can carry its own fine print.

The Pact ends with the scouts leaving camp for the last time, unsure as to what is to come.

April finished the book and dropped it on her lap.

Ripley, who had long ago stopped cartwheeling and had been sitting and listening to April read aloud, clapped her hands to her cheeks.

"That's Deborah the ghost? And Daedalus?" she gasped.

"I think so," April said, scrambling to her feet. "Let's go find Mal and Molly!"

"Yeah," Ripley said, bouncing next to April. "Wow, this is the longest ghost story!"

And it wasn't over yet.

CHAPTER 27

Sometimes being a good scout means supporting a friend, even if that friend is lecturing about something that freaks you out on a good day.

Sitting in a warehouse full of soggy hooks and ropes, with rows and rows of upside-down boats dripping dry in the corner, Mal was jittery.

Mal and Molly had woken late and so rushed to make Barney's lecture covering 102 keys to boating safety, which meant there was no time to talk about Claudia or ghosts or anything else.

At least not until Barney was finished explaining the nuances of boating safety. A subject Mal was only sort of happy to learn about, hoping it wouldn't be something she would ever have to use.

"The most important thing," Barney said, their face squished against their life preserver, "is to remember that the safest practice on the water is the same as on land, which is the buddy system.

"Have the right gear." Barney held up a finger. "Be prepared." They held up another finger. "And be prepared for the worst."

Mal gulped.

"Being prepared for the worst means you're ready when things go south." Barney smiled. "But hopefully you'll have smooth sailing. That's your water safety lecture for the day. Thanks, everyone!"

As the crowd of now more knowledgeable scouts filtered out of the boating shed, April and Ripley stood by the door with Jo.

Jo had been literally yanked out of her workshop by April and so her hands were still covered in grease. She rubbed her palms on the wood of the boat house, attempting to remove at least a layer of grime. "So, what was so urgent?"

April held up *The Pact*. "Another piece of the puzzle. Which I will share when—"

Mal and Molly appeared at the door.

"What are you doing here?" Mal asked, noting that April was practically bouncing with anticipation.

"April found this supercool book," Ripley gushed.

"It's about Daedalus and how they became the ghost cabin!" April added, waving the book.

"Deborah wrote it," Ripley said.

"See," April said as Roanoke gathered around, "they made a wish on something called the Specter's Seal, which, okay, let's just take a moment to take in how cool it is that there's something called the Specter's Seal."

April took a moment.

Molly looked at Mal. "Actually, we also have something we should probably share."

Jo raised an eyebrow. "Do tell."

"It appears that the Mystery of the Missing Socks isn't about how Claudia wanted to help Daedalus get badges," Mal explained. "It's about Claudia needing our help to leave Miss Qiunzella's."

"Wait." April looked down. "That's not in the book."

"We just found out," Mal said. "Like last night."

"She *can't* leave?" Ripley asked.

"No," Molly said.

Mal tried to study Molly's face, but it was hard because she was looking at the ground.

"Do we know how to help her?" Jo, always practical, asked.

Mal shook her head. "She just said she couldn't do it without us."

"Well, if we want answers," Ripley said, "we can go talk to Deborah, right? I mean, she wrote the book."

Jo considered Heddie's words in the shop. "Something tells me this is going to be complicated."

Molly looked up. "I think you're right."

"The most complicated ghost story EVER," Ripley gasped as they headed to the mess hall, "and it all started with SOCKS!"

153

PART THREE

FACE YOUR FEARS

THE SCOUT IN THE MIRROR

In the dark of night and the light of day, the world is full of things for scouts to be afraid of. From the tiniest spider to the force of the weather, the world is a place full of hazards and haunting elements.

If we let them, the things we are afraid of can be the things that control us, that get in the way of being the best scouts we can be.

Whether it's standing in the dark, or stepping into the light, for scouts, the challenge is not to erase fears, but to face them.

By facing those things that scare us, the things that seem too big or too much, we face our challenges head-on. By facing the fears that haunt us, we open up the possibility of . . .

CHAPTER 28

A group of bats is called a cauldron. If you have more than one buzzard it's a wake. A collective of ravens is referred to as an unkindness, although I'm sure ravens don't always enjoy that.

A gathering of ghosts has been referred to as many things. A "fright" is one. Most commonly, a "haunting." "Scary" is another word people sometimes use.

"Terrifying" also works.

This is in part because, when ghosts are angry, it's like a thunderstorm, but with dead people flying around the room.

(Incidentally, fear of lightning, which none of the members of Roanoke experiences, is called astraphobia.)

Roanoke stood in the corner and tried not to look freaked out while the fright of ghosts that resided at Daedalus cabin had a very intense, let's call it, "cabin meeting."

After hearing what Mal and Molly had to say about their recent discoveries, Deborah opened things up with "HOW DARE YOU INTERFERE IN THE BUSINESS OF THE DEAD!"

When ghosts are angry, some shoot green sparks out of their eyes. Some ghosts make a breaking-glass-like screeching noise that seems to come from someplace both far away and very close at the same time.

Deborah could do both.

"We're not trying to interfere," April said. "I mean, really *we*, maybe *I*, can be interfering, I'll give you that, but I swear on a stack of Lemonade Stand series that this time—"

Mal stepped forward. "Claudia asked us for help."

"CLAUDIA!" Little green flames shot out of the top of Deborah's phantasmal crown of hair, which was sticking straight up.

Though Roanoke was certainly trying, it was hard to seem calm in the wake of Deborah's fury, especially when Bubbles was so full of panicked static he was practically a puffball.

"What the Brittany Williams have we gotten ourselves into?" April whispered.

Somewhere in this hurricane, Mal looked at Molly. Molly seemed transfixed, caught in Deborah and Claudia's tractor beam of rage.

"I didn't know," Claudia said from between gritted teeth, "what I was promising. I didn't know I was promising FOREVER, Deborah. I didn't know what FOREVER would be."

"You're trying to get away from us," Deborah snapped. "You made a PACT, Claudia, A PROMISE, to ALL OF US."

"Claudia." Heddie took Claudia's hand. "We want to understand."

"NO!" Deborah screamed, breaking their grip. "We DO NOT."

There was a snap of what felt like a hundred volts of ghost rage. It rang Roanoke's eardrums. It made all the hairs on everyone's arms stand up.

"Oh, Claudia." Deborah sank to the ground. Like a balloon that suddenly doesn't have enough air in it to be a balloon anymore.

"What the cauliflower, Claudia," Maggie fumed. "What could you possibly want to see that's better than this place?"

There was a pause. A space in the fury. Claudia looked at Mal.

"New York?" Her voice wavered.

"NEW YORK?!" Heddie tossed her hands in the air. "Good LEEK, Claudia!"

Jo, who had also been to New York, could see Claudia's point, but also thought Austin was pretty nice.

Claudia dropped down to the floor. Floated over to Deborah. "Tell me," she said.

Deborah didn't look at her. "Tell you what?"

"I know how it works, Deborah. I know the Seal can only grant a wish to the living. All I need is for you to tell me where it is," Claudia pleaded.

"That's what you want," Deborah said, pointing at Roanoke. "That's why you pulled them in? Not to help us. To help you."

"Tell me where it is," Claudia repeated, face-to-face with Deborah. "Where is the Specter's Seal?"

The cabin trembled like it was teetering on a subway platform.

"Deborah." Heddie slipped forward. "Just . . ."

"Well, I don't know where the Seal is," Deborah spat. "So you're trapped, Claudia. My sincerest apologies."

April covered her mouth to muffle a gasp. Molly looked at Mal while trying to keep a grip on Bubbles, who was just getting puffier and puffier.

"For decades now," Deborah said, looking up from her puddle of ghost on the floor, "you have painted a sacred pact as a prison sentence."

"I didn't lead the life you lived," Claudia boomed. "I spent my life in a single town in a house making ends meet. There are things I want to see!"

There is very little sadder than phantasmal tears, streaks of light that tremble down the cheeks of ghosts. Deborah's face was suddenly flooded with a soft light.

Heddie and Maggie floated over to Deborah. Cradled her in their arms.

"I thought you were better, I thought you cared about this cabin, about US." Deborah looked up at Claudia with green glowing eyes. "But you DON'T. All you care about is YOURSELF. You're not a LUMBERGHOST. You are but a ghost of the scout I knew."

Molly put her hands to her mouth, like she was trying to stifle whatever was about to come out.

April stumbled backward. "Oh my gosh."

And with that, Claudia stormed, which is to say, flew, out of the cabin.

After a few moments of a silent standoff between Daedalus and Roanoke, April, Jo, Ripley, Mal, and Molly all left as well.

By the time they got back to Roanoke, Jen was anxiously waiting outside.

"Where have you BEEN?" she gasped, throwing her hands in the air. "It's nearly midnight!"

For once, Roanoke was quiet, their minds all busy with a flurry of questions, four tiny snow globes of busy thoughts preparing for bed while Jen paced.

"Right to bed." Jen frowned. "No ifs, ands, or buts, you scouts."

"Sorry, Jen." Ripley slipped under the covers. "We were just . . ."

"Helping out some fellow scouts," Jo finished.

Mal looked at Molly curled up in her bunk.

"All right," Jen said, her hand hovering by the light switch. "Well, get some sleep and tomorrow you can be even more helpful."

Mal hoped that was true.

CHAPTER 29

The next day, after breakfast and a cross-country run, April called a very necessary cabin meeting in a clearing in the woods.

April paced. "THIS is a VERY NECESSARY cabin meeting! The Mystery of the Missing Sock is now officially a phantom debacle and we need to figure out what to do next."

Ripley wiggled her toes in her toe socks from her perch in the tree above April. "Agreed."

"Okay," Jo said, leaning against a tall pine, "what do we know?"

"First! We go over the facts." April held up her notes. "Noting that *The Pact* is a work of fiction but based on a very real thing because we've MET the scouts of Daedalus, I propose we treat the details inside as facts."

"Agreed," Jo said, "in THIS case."

April held up a finger. "Fact number one: Many many MANY years ago, the (then living) scouts of Daedalus made a wish on something called the Specter's Seal. And that wish is the reason they are Lumberghosts today."

"Check." Ripley nodded, still wiggling.

Mal and Molly also nodded, without wiggling. Molly sat against another pine, cuddling Bubbles in her lap. Mal stood over Molly, her arms crossed over her chest.

"According to Claudia," Jo said, "to set her free, we need to make a wish with the Seal."

"I mean, yeah," April said, looking at her well-detailed and carefully penned bullet points. "Unless there's another wish stone thing out there, let's say finding the Seal is our shortest route to getting Claudia out of camp. BUT we don't know where the Seal is."

April pulled a pen out of her pocket. "Let's make that Fact Two."

"Did *The Pact* have any clues in it?" Ripley asked.

"Not really," April said. "In *The Pact*, the scouts had to give the Seal back, but it doesn't say where it ended up. Fact 3B."

"So, first thing is, we need to find out where the Seal is now." Jo held up four fingers. "Which I say means library research, maybe asking the other Daedalus scouts, maybe someone could talk to Deborah again?"

Ripley's eyes went wide. "I don't know. Deborah looked really sad."

Fact 4.

Molly held up her hand, not high, just high enough so April noticed.

"I was just thinking." Molly paused. "I mean, if we do this, we're sort of Un-Lumberghosting, right?"

Fact 5?

Now Ripley stopped wiggling. "Hey, that's kind of sad."

"But it's what she wants," April added, "right, Mal?"

Fact 6?

"I mean . . ." Mal looked at Molly, who was cuddling Bubbles's face close to her cheek, something she only did when she was really sad. "I think so."

Fact 7?

Jo looked up at the position of the sun in the sky. "For now, I'm going to Barney's final lecture on Water Ski safety, but after that, I'll head to the library and see if I can find anything about the Seal there."

"April and I have our Berry Delicious pies and jams badge to work on," Ripley said, swinging down from the tree.

"But we'll be BERRY happy to talk to the other scouts tonight," April added, pleased to finally use a berry pun, which was one of the main reasons she was doing the badge.

Mal peered over at Molly. "Maybe we'll talk to Deborah," she said, her voice high and unsure.

"Sure, tonight." Molly stood as Bubbles climbed up onto her head. "I have some reading to do."

With that, Roanoke scattered off to the corners of the camp, leaving Mal behind, alone in the trees.

Mal watched Molly walk off into the forest, the dapple of sunlight catching her hair.

Molly hadn't really said anything to Mal since they'd left the Daedalus cabin. It was like Mal was still in the dark.

Fact 8: Mal was worried. About Molly.

CHAPTER 30

What requires twenty cartons of strawberries and twelve bags of sugar to complete?

Two guesses.

First hint, it involves April, and Ripley.

If you guessed the Berry Delicious badge, you would be right. If you were in the process of GETTING your Berry Delicious badge, you would be very sticky.

"All my fingers are glued together," Ripley trilled happily, waving her hands in front of her. "With SUGAR!"

"I'm pretty happy with our jams," April said, looking at their display. "I'm going to call this one The Last Strawberry and this one is . . ."

"Once in a Blueberry Moon?" Ripley offered.

"Great gobs of Christina Tosi!" April's eyes popped open with the sudden realization of the task before her, naming a blueberry jam.

PUN CITY!

"It could be Out of the Blueberry Jam. It could be True Blueberry, Baby I Love Jam. It could be Blueberry Monday, Blueberry Jam Is Not My Lover, Still Got the Blueberries . . ." Thin wisps of smoke seemed to be spiraling out of April's ears. "It could be—"

PUN OVERLOAD!

"Hey!" BunBun appeared in front of the table with a spoon, bright blue pom-poms perched on her head. "Are you ready for your jam tasting or are you just having pun over here?"

"We're ready for tasting." Ripley adjusted her apron and scooped her hair, which was also blue, out of her face. "But we haven't named the jams yet."

"That's okay, you don't have to name a jam. It's not a person." BunBun whipped a shiny silver spoon from her apron, dipped it into the small blueberry-filled pot in front of April, who was still whispering puns to herself, and dabbled a dollop on her tongue.

Ripley watched as BunBun appeared to savor and consider the jam, rolling it on her tongue while making loud smacking sounds.

"Good texture, good mouth feel, good flavor, good berry representation," BunBun said, adding a final smack. "Very good."

"Berry good?" April grinned.

BunBun slid her spoon into her apron. "Can I borrow some for later?"

Just then Ripley had a thought.

"Is it for you," she asked, "or for the ghost?"

April looked at Ripley. "Ghost?"

Ripley had been thinking since they'd started adding sugar to heaps of fruit that BunBun had mentioned a ghost at the campfire a few nights ago, but it didn't seem like it was Daedalus, or Daedalus probably would have mentioned something. So . . .

"It's for the ghost," Bunbun answered.

"You can take the jam," Ripley said, leaning on the table, "if we can talk to the ghost."

"You can meet the ghost," BunBun said, pinging her pom-poms with a flick of her finger, "if I can name the jam."

"Deal." Ripley held out her hand.

BunBun shook it, vigorously.

"Wait." April looked at her pot of unnamed masterpiece. "What are you naming it?"

"This jam is named Levy," BunBun said. "See you tonight! Mess hall. Nine P.M. SHARP."

"Levy?" April squeaked as BunBun bounced over to the next table. "That's not even a pun."

"But maybe we'll get more ghost facts," Ripley said, holding up a finger, "and we can always make and name more jam."

April grabbed a carton of raspberries and a pot. "Fine. Then let's get started on Raspberry Hooray."

Raspberry Hooray isn't quite as cool as Rhapsody in Blueberry, but sometimes a scout must make sacrifices.

CHAPTER 31

Mal was supposed to be practicing guitar, but the music just wasn't in her that day. So instead she wandered around looking for Molly until she spotted Jen and an able crew of hammering scouts working to repair one of the roofs recently damaged by a set of very sharp griffin claws.

Stacks of fallen feathers had already been collected and turned into pillows. And, I will say, if you've never slept on a pillow made with griffin feathers (which are only acceptable to use if you have a bunch of them left in your camp after a griffin swarm), you haven't slept.

Mal hadn't really slept all that much over the past few days, which had very little to do with her pillow, and everything to do with her worries.

A small crew of scouts was hammering away on the roof tiles and on their Because I Have a Hammer badge. A badge that teaches scouts the basics of hammer, nail, screw, drill, and, inadvertently, roofs.

"Mal," Jen called down, slinging her hammer into her pocket. "Shouldn't you be in the music portable?"

Jumping down from the roof, Jen raised an eyebrow. "Not that you scouts are ever where you're supposed to be."

Mal considered. "I'd say sixty-five percent of the time we are."

"Hmmmm. Okay. I'd say sixty," Jen said, brushing the sawdust off her sleeves. "But it's a guess. Did you find your socks?"

"I did." Mal held out her feet, which were now socked.

"You don't look very pleased," Jen noted, lowering her face to look closer at Mal. "Everything okay?"

"I just worry." Mal shrugged. "About people. Sometimes."

"OH!" Jen held her hands up in the air. "TELL ME ABOUT IT! Imagine worrying about five scouts who are

ALWAYS off on crazy adventures that probably put them in the path of DANGER, like possibly in the claws of giant griffins or on the backs of mountains that don't exist."

"That sounds very stressful," Mal said.

"It is. BUT." Jen held up a stern finger. "The key to being a good counselor is knowing that worrying doesn't actually do anything. Which is very frustrating, as you can imagine, but it is the truth."

Just then, in addition to the noise of hammering, there was a very loud creak. The hammering abruptly stopped.

"OH! GOTTA GO!" Jen cried, dashing off toward the cabin. "HOW MANY SCOUTS ARE ON THE ROOF? I SAID FOUR!"

Several scouts pointed at one another.

"Which one of us is five?" Marcie from Dighton called down.

"It's not me," Leah said, pulling out a nail. "I'm three."

"I'M three," Caitlyn of Roswell piped in. "You're TWO. Wait, or are you one?"

Jen waved her arms. "Everyone DOWN!"

Mal turned and started walking toward the library.

Worrying wasn't doing anything but eating at her stomach.

Mal was sure there was something else she could do to make things better, she just didn't know what.

CHAPTER 32

One of the most common fears among non-scouts is arachnophobia, which is the fear of spiders.

A fear of spiders is an easy thing to explain, because a spider, while not actually menacing (most spiders, as scouts with their I Spider badge know, are harmless and generally contribute to pest control) are a little scary because they have eight legs and that's more than most things.

Some fears are not as easy to explain.

In part because some fears, like the fear that there will never be enough cheese for everyone who wants it, the fear that aliens have no sense of humor, and the fear that bell-bottoms will one day become popular again and become everyone's pant of choice, do not have an official phobia name.

In part because some fears, many fears, are just a feeling. A rotten feeling like a rotten cucumber someone has to fish out of the fridge and throw out.

Molly had everything that she needed in front of her to do math. For two days now, she'd taken the books out of her mother's package and placed them in front of her. And for two days now she'd sat staring at the pages.

Doing nothing.

Partly because of a feeling in her stomach like a rotten cucumber, a feeling she'd had since she watched Deborah in the cabin the night before.

Sitting under a pine tree, with her math book open to page 112 on her lap, and Bubbles snoozing on her head, Molly pulled out her pencil and stared at the numbers on the page and tried not to think about Daedalus. And the fact that Claudia was asking them to help her do the one thing Molly was truly afraid of doing . . .

Leaving.

Molly thought about last night in the cabin when Deborah sank to the ground and cried, about what it must feel like to be Deborah. To lose a friend, something that scared Molly more than spiders or lakes or anything that anyone else could be afraid of.

Molly often thought about the fact that Mal had a whole world on the other side of the camp gates. And all Molly had was . . .

Homework.

Secretly, which is to say, in a way Molly couldn't make herself say out loud, it made Molly not want to help Claudia. It made Molly want to yell at Claudia that she was the luckiest ghost in the world. That Molly would give anything to make a wish like that, a wish that would keep her at Miss Qiunzella's . . . forever.

Molly stared at her textbook. While she was thinking about Claudia, she'd been drawing, drawing right on top of the math problems she was supposed to be solving.

Molly blinked.

Sometimes when Molly was distracted, she drew circles in circles. Little mazes.

Labyrinths.

Partly because Molly was kind of a Greek mythology nut.

The story of the Labyrinth in Greek mythology was the story of a maze built to house a creature called the Minotaur. A maze built by . . .

Daedalus.

Just then there was a rustling in the bushes, and Mal appeared.

"Hey," Mal said carefully, holding out a carefully wrapped sandwich. "You missed dinner."

"Yeah." Molly frowned. "I guess I got a little distracted."

"By the Mystery of the Specter's Seal," Mal asked, "or by math?"

"Mostly the mystery," Molly said. "I just had this thought, I don't know, maybe it's nothing."

"I doubt it's nothing," Mal said, sitting down next to Molly.

"Just." Molly took a small bite of sandwich. "It's interesting. That Daedalus found the Seal in a labyrinth. In Greek mythology, Daedalus BUILT the Labyrinth."

"Huh." Mal tilted her head. "Coincidence?"

"I don't know." Molly sighed. "I guess I don't really have anything."

"Maybe to solve the mystery you just need some more information." Mal stood. "How do you feel about talking to another ghost?"

"I feel like I could talk to another ghost." Molly held out her hand and Mal hoisted her up.

"To the kitchen," Mal trumpeted.

"A kitchen ghost?" Molly asked, leaving her books behind.

"April said we're paying a pot of jam to see her," Mal explained.

"How perfectly Lumberweird." Molly smiled.

It would be.

CHAPTER 33

Of all the ghosts that populate the afterlife, kitchen ghosts are probably the silliest. At night, they bang on the pots and pans with wooden spoons, so that people listening spend many hours wondering if it is the wind.

Generally, it's ghosts.

If you don't feed kitchen ghosts, they will switch your sugar for salt and your flour for sand and all kinds of other things that will make your food taste terrible. Kitchen ghosts view messing with people as a job of sorts. A calling.

Kitchen ghosts rarely get invited to parties because of this switcheroo silliness, but kitchen ghosts also see their afterlife as a sort of party and so they don't really care.

There were only a handful of people who knew about Miss Qiunzella's kitchen ghost. Kzyzzy, obviously, had had many encounters with Inez, including one switcheroo that resulted in the invention of her savory pancake special. And there was Rosie, who sometimes liked to take a nettle tea with Inez and reminisce about old times. Bearwoman knew about Inez but found her a nuisance and disagreed with her insistence on vegetarianism.

And, of course, there was BunBun, who was in charge of making sure Inez got her offerings of delicious goodies. BunBun was probably Inez's current favorite semi-scout, because BunBun took Inez's eating habits quite seriously. Because BunBun took everything quite seriously.

It was for BunBun that Inez agreed to talk to April, Ripley, Mal, and Molly, and for jam. Because Inez was a HUGE fan of jam.

And April and Ripley made great jam.

"We used castor sugar," April explained.

"And lavender," Ripley added. "And a splash of lemon."

Unlike the ghosts of Daedalus, Inez looked like an old woman, maybe eighty (but she'd been eighty for a long long time). She wore an apron and a puffy-sleeved dress. She did not look like she had any teeth. Her hair was long and twisted into a bun the size of a family loaf. Also, no shoes or socks. Inez actually didn't really like socks. Never had.

Mal tried to decide what Inez reminded her of. She looked a bit like a ghost and also a little bit like a muffin. A ghost muffin.

"Did you know Daedalus?" April asked.

"Aie! Those wee scampers," Inez tutted, "messin' with tha witches' tings. No goood!"

"After they took the Seal," Molly asked, "what happened?"

"Whell, tha di-rector whas FURDIOUS! And they had to give tha Seal bak, didn' they?" Inez smacked her lips covered in jam. Which was kind of odd. Like watching globs of jam float in midair.

"What happened to it?" Ripley asked.

"Aie! They put ee bak!" Inez rocked back in her chair.

"Back in the labyrinth?" Molly asked.

Inez nodded, sticking her finger back in the jam. "Wher else?"

"Where is the labyrinth?" Mal asked.

"HA! Don you wanna know. Iz DEEP BELOW." Inez narrowed her eyes. "Wher wee scampers whod nay find it agin."

"Deep below?" April looked at Mal and Molly.

"In the DEEPS, lass." Inez waggled her significant eyebrows.

"The deeps." The wheels inside Mal's head churned.

"Where no one could get to it," Molly whispered.

"Aye." Inez grinned. "Was quite a sight. A whol' production. Rain for DAYS. And then, the perfect hiding place. Right under yar noses. An now, ah'll be off."

And with that, Inez dunked her ghost finger in the jam, popped it in her mouth, and in a puff of what looked like smoke but was not, disappeared.

"Did that help?" BunBun asked, sticking a piece of toast in what was left of Levy.

Ripley looked at April. "Maybe?"

"I have an idea," Molly said.

"So do I." Mal grabbed Molly's hand.

"What's deep?" Molly asked Mal as they headed out of the mess hall. "What's deep and can be MADE?"

"To the library, I'm assuming," April said.

"To the library," Mal and Molly said together.

CHAPTER 34

As Barney, who had their Take It or Lake It badge, knew, lakes are fabulously complex and interesting things. They can be found anywhere, vary in depth and size, and are mostly freshwater. Some lakes shake the hands of rivers; some, like Lake Specter, do not. Some lakes were made by people, some lakes were created by volcanoes. Some by glaciers.

And some lakes, Molly knew, thanks to Barney's many lectures on water safety and water-related subjects, are made by people.

"My guess: The labyrinth is in a lake," Molly said as they gathered in the library with Jo, who was surrounded by books, scrolls, and maps.

"A Lumberjane-made lake," Mal added.

"You think they just poured a lake on top of a labyrinth?" April asked. "To hide it?"

"Makes sense, given we're sitting in a library that's actually a ship in the middle of camp," Mal noted.

"It also explains a cartographic inconsistency," Jo said, pointing at the map she had laid out on the table.

"When the camp was first established," Jo explained, "Miss Qiunzella commissioned a map of the entire camp's geographical features. Including surrounding forests and mountains, et cetera."

April leaned over the table, appreciating such a sensible move.

"Very detailed," she marveled. April liked a good map.

"Note here, right outside Wiggly Woods." Jo pointed. "The cartographers listed this area as 'dangerous terrain' with an added note from Miss Qiunzella that it was off limits to scouts."

"Maybe trying to keep them away from magical stuff?" Ripley asked.

"Maybe. Because, then, twenty years later, they commissioned another map, the map we use now." Jo rolled out another map on top of the first. "Now, in this same area, instead of 'dangerous terrain,' there are several lakes, including . . ."

Jo pointed to a small blue blob on the map. "The lake we know as Lake Specter."

"Okay." April nodded. "I'm feeling better and better about our jam trade."

"What better place to hide something as big as a labyrinth than in a lake?" Molly asked. "The Specter's Seal must be at the bottom of Lake Specter."

"Also, interesting note," Mal said, pointing at the first map, "Daedalus wasn't always ON a lake."

"Of course." April traced the little squares representing the scouts' tents on the first map with her finger. "They would have been with all the other cabins. Which weren't even cabins. They were tents!"

"Also," Jo said. "Lake Specter. Specter's Seal."

"So the labyrinth is 'right under thar noses,'" Molly realized. "Like Inez said."

"Do Daedalus *know* they're on top of the labyrinth?" Ripley asked.

"They might not," Jo said. "The lake could have been created after they left. This map was drawn twenty years after they'd gone."

"I feel like if any of them would know, it would be Deborah," Molly said.

"It's dark out," Jo said. "So, there's one way to find out."

187

Maybe ghosts have super hearing. Or maybe Deborah was floating somewhere in the dark while Inez ate her jam and spilled the beans to April and Ripley.

Either way, she was waiting when Roanoke got to Daedalus cabin. Heddie and Maggie floated behind her. Claudia was nowhere to be seen.

April stepped forward. "We know where the Seal is."

"You know nothing," Deborah snapped, spinning around the cabin in a streak of white light, her skirts billowing.

"Tell us then," Mal said, stepping up next to Molly. "Tell us what we don't know. Help us."

"The Seal is not yours to meddle with." Deborah's eyes glowed green.

"But you did," Jo pointed out. "You made a wish."

"A wish is not a simple thing," Heddie said.

"BE QUIET." Deborah spun around, nose to nose with Heddie.

"What the juniper berries!" Maggie yelped. "Deborah!"

"We want to understand," April began.

"UNDERSTAND THIS," Deborah growled, turning to face the scouts. "If you do this, if you help her, you will be taking her away from us. FOREVER. If she leaves . . ."

Molly reached her hand out, without looking away from Deborah, and grabbed Mal's.

"If she leaves . . ." Deborah floated up, the air trembled.

Molly squeezed Mal's hand hard.

"She can never come back."

CHAPTER 35

A bonfire is a whole lot less comforting when you've got a huge problem to solve. While the rest of the scouts of Miss Qiunzella's munched on marshmallows and sang acoustic versions of various songs, Roanoke stewed.

"So what do we do?" April sat on her log, head in hands.

"I mean." Jo considered. "If the Seal is at the bottom of the lake, we CAN get to it. We have the technology. With Heddie's help, and with Barney's water safety know-how, and the water gear we used last time April went into a lake, we have everything we need."

"It's kind of what we DO," April said, throwing her hands up. "Am I right?"

Mal looked at Molly, who once again had folded into herself. Like she did when she was sad. She was sitting on a log and looking at the fire, but it was like part of her was so far away.

"If we don't do it," Ripley reasoned, "Claudia will be sad. If we do, Deborah will be sad."

"Probably Heddie and Maggie will be sad, too," Molly said quietly.

"That's true," April groaned. "What the Beth Ditto, you guys?"

Mal looked over at Molly. "Maybe we shouldn't do it."

Jo turned with a start. "Really?"

"I mean," Mal said. "I mean, Claudia made a pact, a promise. And we're sort of helping her break that promise, right?"

"I guess." April sunk into her log. "That doesn't feel right, though."

"It just doesn't feel very SCOUT," Jo said.

Just then Mal felt a hand on her back. It was Molly.

"Because it's not," Molly said. "It's not the Lumberjane thing to do. Claudia asked for our help. Maybe in a weird way, but she asked. And even if she made a promise, WE made a promise when we became Lumberjanes."

"But," Mal said quietly, "Deborah said she won't be able to come back."

"Well," Molly said, "that's Claudia's choice."

"You know." April wiggled her fingers in the air. "That does feel like the thing to do."

"So now all we need is a plan." Molly looked at Mal. "Got one?"

"Well," Mal said, unsure. "Yeah, I think I do."

"I bet you do." Molly smiled.

Just then there was a whisper from the shadows.

"PSST! Hey!"

Ripley swiveled. "HEY!"

"Looks like you turnips are going to need our help," the voice growled.

CHAPTER 36

PLAN #4586.

April and Ripley had finals for their Fruity Pies and were off in the mess hall so as not to tip off Jen, who was judging and expecting April and Ripley's Everything's Peachy Pie.

At Lake Specter, Jo and Heddie were in charge of rigging equipment. Fortunately, Jo had had the brilliant idea of using Heddie's technical skills to find wiring to update April's scuba suit, a design she'd whipped up on a moment's notice and was never pleased with. Now the suit was equipped with a breathing apparatus (no more long tube) and a helmet with a spotlight.

Mal was in charge of not freaking out.

"Okay. Dark water"—she gulped, pointing while standing a solid five feet back from the water's edge—"you . . . do not scare me. Please do not swallow Molly forever."

"Mal. Headlamp." Molly pointed as she strapped on the scuba gear. "We've got ghost scuba technology designed by Heddie. Plus, Claudia is coming with me. It's going to be fine."

"We'll monitor you from above," Jo said, pointing at a tiny silver box, which pinged with Molly's vitals that were read from a tiny sensor on Molly's wrist also developed by Jo and Heddie.

"Can ghosts swim?" Mal looked at Claudia.

"Ghosts can be in the water. I would not call it swimming. Mostly we can breathe underwater because," Heddie noted, "we don't have to breathe."

"Something about this." Mal shook her head. "Something I don't like. Also, WATER."

"I don't know if this helps, but Heddie said Daedalus has never seen a weird sea creature or dragon or other scary thing in a few hundred years of being on this lake," Jo said, patting Mal's back. "Plus, thanks to Barney's input, we've got a pretty solid water safety list going."

Molly rubbed spit on the glass of her goggles, which is gross but useful. "I'm going to go down, get the Seal," she said, "and come right back up."

Mal put her hand on Molly's arm. "You know you don't have to do this, right?"

"I want to," Molly said, pulling the goggles over her head.

"Are you sure?" Mal picked up Molly's hand, which was already cold.

"Yes," Molly said. "It's what you would do, Mal. If you weren't scared of water, right? You would help Claudia. Because it's the Lumberjane thing to do."

Mal squeezed Molly's hand. "Please do not let anything bad happen to you."

"I'll try," Molly said, and with that, trailed by Claudia, she marched through the line of cattails and other lake plants and into the lake.

Watching Molly sink into the water made Mal feel like her heart was sinking into her shoes.

"Well," Jo said, throwing a few switches on her and Heddie's air pump system, "let's see if we're right about the Seal."

Molly was up to her waist in the water. It was cold. Very cold. The water soaked her socks, which she'd forgotten to take off. Her legs pricked with goose bumps.

"Molly?" Claudia was up to her neck in the lake.

"Yes?" Molly's voice was muffled by her mouthpiece.

"Thank you," Claudia said.

195

"You're welcome," Molly said. "Claudia, I know what it means to be someplace you don't want to be."

Molly switched on her headlamp. "Ready?"

"Ready," Claudia said.

Molly slipped into the depths of Lake Specter.

CHAPTER 37

L ake Specter, made by magic, was not like most lakes.
For one, it was fish-free. As Molly's face slipped
below into the darkness of the lake, she noticed how
still the water was. Not a blip. Not even those teeny-tiny
fish that swim in little silvery schools. It was almost like a
dream, thick and black except for the spotlight created by
her headlamp.

It was hard to see how deep they were sinking. It felt
like the world just kept falling and falling out from under
them. Every time she reached down with her foot, it swung
in the emptiness. Again and again, until, finally, after what
felt like forever, but was not, Molly's foot touched the soft,
unfortunately squishy bottom of the lake.

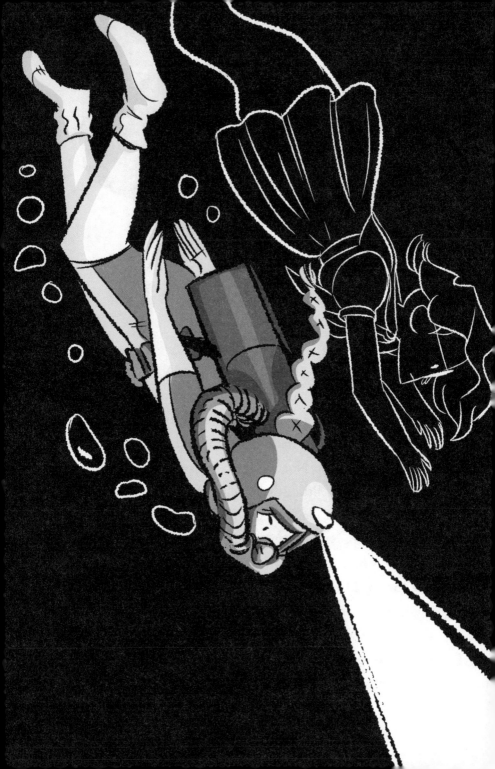

Claudia looked at Molly, who was slowly turning, taking in her surroundings, waiting for her light to catch something. Something other than nothing, which seemed to be all around them.

A halo of bubbles burbled up from her mouthpiece.

Molly shone her light on Claudia. Who shrugged.

And then, just beyond Claudia's shifting form, Molly spotted it.

A wall in the middle of the bottom of the lake.

Like a castle in the middle of nowhere.

Which briefly made Molly think of her mother's fishbowl and its tiny fortress with a drawbridge their goldfish, Mr. Goldfish, swam in and out of.

This was like a very gothic version of that.

Molly kicked toward the wall. The icy water was already turning her fingertips numb as she placed her hand on the stony surface. It was bumpy, covered with something small and sharp, like a thousand tiny clams.

"Is this the labyrinth?" Claudia asked, knowing Molly could not hear her. It looked different, although, honestly, the last time she saw it was a long time ago.

"TURN BACK, CLAUDIA!"

"Deborah." Claudia whirled around to see Deborah, whose eyes were blazing jade green.

The sudden appearance of Deborah scared the bubbles out of Molly, who fell back with a "BUBBBLLLAA!"

Ghosts, of course, can talk underwater; people cannot. Ghosts can also YELL underwater. Which is just as unpleasant underwater as it is on land.

"DON'T you DARE move another inch," Deborah barked, swimming in front of Claudia. "What the cauliflower do you think you're doing?"

"You know exactly what I'm doing," Claudia said, pushing past Molly. "My *friends* are helping me get the Seal. Which *you* kept secret from me!"

"I thought it was pretty obvious," Deborah said with a glare. "But then maybe I was the smart scout of Daedalus."

"You are the BOSSY scout of Daedalus," Claudia sneered. "Heddie is the smart one. GO HOME."

"Home? Really? Funny for YOU to say that," Deborah sniffed. "Since you no longer consider this your final resting place."

"Funny? How about FUNNY to see YOU here since you made it abundantly clear you have no intention of helping me," Claudia snarled. "An eternity of telling me what to do. Some scout you are."

"You're questioning my qualifications as a Lumberghost, when you've dragged these Lumberjanes to the bottom of a lake, scouts that could still DIE," Deborah snapped back. "You are a blight on the Daedalus cabin."

"Well, I won't be for much longer!"

"FINE!"

Molly couldn't hear exactly what either ghost was saying. But she could guess from:

Glub!

Glub glub!

. . . that it wasn't good.

A small current was swirling around Deborah and Claudia, a churning in the water that was pushing against Molly. Molly held out her arms to try to stay upright.

"If you didn't want this you could have said something a hundred years ago!"

"Who could say anything?! If I did, what would you hear?"

"Don't blame ME for your LIES!"

"You don't care about me!"

Deborah threw her arms out with a huge WHOOSH. "I CARE ABOUT YOU SO MUCH!"

A swell slammed against Molly, who waved her arms to try and get her balance.

Ugh, Molly thought, grabbing at the wall behind her.

The wall that was supposed to be behind her.

Which was now . . .

Gone.

"NO, YOU DON'T!" Claudia said, throwing her arms up.

Whoosh.

With a final gust, Molly was tossed backward. She reached out her hands, grazing the edge of a gap in the wall, about the size of a refrigerator door.

"All you care about is DAEDALUS," Claudia seethed.

"YOU ARE DAEDALUS," Deborah snapped.

"Wait." Claudia froze. "Why is it so dark?

"Molly?" Claudia swiveled in the water. "Molly?"

Deep in the heart of Lake Specter, there was only darkness.

CHAPTER 38

Depending on where you are, it can be very hard not to think of something scary.

If you're playing basketball with your friends, or working on a puzzle, or eating pizza in the park, it might be very easy to think only non-scary thoughts.

But there are times it is VERY hard not to think scary thoughts.

Especially if you're scared.

Or if you're standing on the edge of a lake with water blacker than the night sky, waiting for someone you care about to reappear.

If you're standing on the edge of what feels like a black hole, it can be very difficult not to think of scary things.

Water had always made Mal think of scary things, ever since she was a kid and Bang!, her stuffed drum, fell into Lake Marmalade.

Lake Marmalade was the lake next to Mal's nana's cottage. It was named after a dog named Marmalade. It was a big lake with a big dock. The dock that was splintered and knotty with a big rusty ladder on the end. It had what Mal then thought were earrings for tying little paddleboats up.

One day Mal was playing with Bang! on the edge of the lake, the way any budding musician plays with her stuffed drum, working on Patty Schemel's drums from *Live Through This* (Mal's favorite Hole album). This required a lot of kicking, because Bang! was a snare and kick drum, which was all going fine until Mal kicked Bang! harder than she meant to, and Bang! skittered off the dock and into the lake.

Mal would never forget the look on Bang!'s stitched-up face as it disappeared into the water. One of Bang!'s eyes came loose and floated on the lake surface while the rest of Bang! soaked and sank.

Mal screamed so loud that, for a minute, the fish stopped swimming. That's what her grandma said, anyway.

When something fell in the lake, Mal's grandma would say it disappeared into the soggy bottom.

Now Bang! was somewhere in the soggy bottom. Gone.

After that, Mal never went in the lake again.

Mal tried not to think of what was at the bottom of the deep dark lake, but not thinking about it was really hard when there were so many things to think about—sea creatures with weird eyes and teeth, slimy seaweeds with long seaweed arms.

Also, once, Barney told Mal that the ocean was an average of 12,100 feet deep.

That's so many feet!

Mal knew the lake wasn't that deep, but she couldn't stop thinking of Molly, falling and falling.

Jo went between watching Mal pace and watching the little blips that meant Molly was still okay.

"They've been gone for hours," Mal said, her hands clutched together, leaning as far as she dared over the lake.

"They've been gone for . . ." Jo looked at her watch. "Nineteen minutes."

"That's a lot," Mal said, staring at the water, willing Molly's head to surface.

"Time is relative," Jo said. "I'm sure she's okay, Mal."

"Something's gone wrong," Mal said.

Just then, the water's surface trembled, and Deborah and Claudia leaped out of the lake.

"She's gone," Claudia wailed.

"YOU LOST HER?!" Mal shrieked. Her knees felt weak.

"She was there," Deborah explained, slipping through the water toward Mal and Jo. "She was by the wall."

"A wall? Did you find the labyrinth?" Mal was already scrambling back to the equipment laid out next to Jo.

"We found a wa—" Claudia said.

"So she could be in the labyrinth," Mal cut in. "She could be lost in the maze."

"We couldn't see," Deborah admitted. "It was so dark. I am so sorry."

"Did you need more light?" Heddie asked, looking at the spare lamp on the grass next to Jo.

Mal pulled the tank on her back. "I'm going in."

"You?" Jo said with a start. "Mal."

Heddie grabbed her little screwdriver and swirled it around her phantom fingers. "Hold on a moment, I'm going to make a quick adjustment."

"Mal." Jo pulled the strap around Mal's tank tight. "Are you sure?"

"Yes." Mal gritted her teeth. "I have to save her."

"We don't have another monitor," Jo said, looking down at Molly's readings. "If you're down there and something happens . . ."

"Claudia and Deborah are coming with me," Mal said. "Buddy system."

"But what if . . ." Claudia looked at Deborah. "If any-thing else happens."

"WE will find her." Deborah looked at Claudia.

"Yes." Mal looked out over the lake. Somewhere in there was Molly. Molly was not disappeared, she was alive and she needed Mal. "We will."

CHAPTER 39

It can be difficult to predict exactly how and when knowledge will become useful.

This is why it is hard for some people to enjoy algebra or chemistry, because it doesn't seem like it's going to come up outside of the classroom or scout meeting in which it is studied.

Of course, algebra is a way to figure out what something (x) equals, which could be the distance between you and a mountain or the weight of a canoe, and chemistry, as Kzyzzy will tell you, is how people make bread.

Lumberjanes know that it is always better to know as many things as you can about as many things as you can because you never know. Lumberjanes know that all knowledge is useful. If you get into enough adventures, eventually everything is relevant.

Including Greek mythology.

First of all, Greek mythology is great for naming your pets, as anyone with a goldfish named Hermes (the name Molly wanted to give Mr. Goldfish) can tell you.

Second of all, it's fun at parties, as anyone with a pet fish named Hermes would also know.

Third of all, if you are ever lost in a maze, thinking about myths can be very helpful.

Partly because it is hard to be freaked out about being somewhere strange when you are thinking about Greek myths. Whatever is happening to you is probably way better than the things that happened to people in Greek myths.

The story of the Labyrinth is a prime example. The Labyrinth was a twisted maze created by Daedalus to hold the Minotaur, a creature that was half bull, half man. With one exception, people were sent into the Labyrinth to . . .

Die, Molly thought to herself, on what she was sure was her third time around the same turn since she'd realized she was alone in whatever this underwater thing was.

Molly, stop. Molly shook her head. Think of something USEFUL.

Molly stepped forward; the water here was colder, ice. Her light seemed smaller, illuminating a spot in front of her no bigger than a soccer ball. Her light was . . . going out.

Nope. She shook her head again, bubbles wrapping around her face. *Don't think about that*, she chided herself.

Molly looked around. *The labyrinth*, she thought.

It wasn't what Molly had pictured when she'd heard of a labyrinth. For one, it had a ceiling, so she couldn't just float up and out of it, which would have been the one benefit of having a labyrinth underwater.

Molly turned. The walls had no distinct markings, so there was nothing to distinguish one wall from another. Which meant she had no idea if she was going in circles or getting anywhere near either the center or the exit to the maze.

Okay, Molly thought. I'm in a structure from Greek mythology. What would Hercules do?

WWHD?

Just then, Molly had another thought. Not about Hercules, or Daedalus, or the Minotaur (could also be a pet name), but about Ariadne (another good pet name) and her ball of string. The tool that helped Theseus (yet another good pet name) escape the maze.

String, Molly thought, looking down. *I need . . .*

Did you know most socks, especially knitted socks, are essentially made out of string? Fortunately, Molly's socks were ones gifted to her by Barney, and so they were knitted with wool. Molly reached down and rolled off one of her socks.

Barney was an expert knitter, but all socks have a thread you can unknot and pull. Which you should only do if you are trying to unravel them. Which Molly did, with a quick tug.

Well, Molly thought, this might not be a real sock mystery, but there's a sock solution.

Wrapping the wool around one of the tiny shells on the wall, Molly gripped her sock with one hand and slowly floated forward, the wool unspooling as she swam forward.

Her light, which at first had been the size of a volleyball, was narrowing to the size of a baseball. It was getting hard to see.

With her unraveling sock in hand, Molly took a deep breath through her mouthpiece and stepped farther into the maze.

CHAPTER 40

How do you face your fears?

Rosie would say, "Head-on."

Of course, holding her hands out like a superhero, her torch leading the way, as she dove down into the darkness, Mal wasn't thinking about the dark water closing in around her.

Mal had a much bigger thing to be afraid of.

Please, she thought, her stomach tightening, *please be okay.*

Deborah and Claudia swirled around her like ghostly fireflies, keeping close to the light and searching the lake bottom for signs of a scout.

Mal could feel her heart thumping in her ears.

She thought about Molly's sunny face, the way she bit her bottom lip when she was playing the accordion, the way she frowned when she got a wrong note in a way that looked like she was burping.

Just then Mal's spotlight caught a patch of gray.

Claudia swam in front of her, waving, then dove down, leading the way, streaking along the tunnel of Mal's light.

With adjustments by Heddie and her tiny screwdriver, Mal's headlight was much brighter than Molly's, which made it much easier to see the labyrinth wall, covered in really creepy toothy-looking things.

Like a tomb, Mal thought.

Great.

Don't think about that, Mal thought.

The outside wall was clearly rounded, like the base of a giant can of soup that had been underwater for longer than most people could remember. Mal looked up, but all her light could catch was black.

It was Deborah who found the door and lead Mal to a hole in the wall not much taller than a Molly.

Without hesitating, Mal plunged inside.

The labyrinth was long and twisty, claustrophobic, with walls that seemed to close in on Mal as she pushed deeper into the maze. The corridors were as narrow as they were infinite. They switched back and back, left and right.

With every kick, Mal could feel the wall hitting her knees and feet.

I'm going to get lost, Mal thought, pulling to a halt. Claudia and Deborah paused, looking confused.

Claudia waved, pointing back to where they had come, then shrugging as if to say, "That way?"

Mal shook her head.

She needed to think.

There was something about a maze, Mal thought, looking at the walls, something she needed to remember. Up close she could see that what she had thought were teeth (UGH) were actually stones (PHEW).

What would Molly think? Mal wondered. If she was here, what would Molly be thinking?

It's a labyrinth! Mal looked around. So, she would be thinking about Greek myths and . . .

Mal pressed her eyes shut. What did Molly say was the thing about the Labyrinth? Something about Hercules? No . . .

Ariadne's thread!

Mal turned to face the wall. She ran her hands along the surface (*Ugh ugh, still feels like teeth, gross gross*), until her hand hit what was undeniably . . . yarn. Bright white. Just like the socks Molly had been wearing. The end of the yarn was tied to one of the more prominent stones.

"MOLLY, YOU GENIUS!" Mal burbled, almost losing her mouthpiece.

Waving wildly, Mal scrambled, whirling her arms in the water, paddling as fast as she could, following the yarn as it twisted along the wall.

All around her was a whooshing silence. All Mal could hear was her own pleading thoughts.

Please be here, please please.

The walls took a sharp turn and, suddenly, the space opened. It was a room. A large round room. Unlike the walls of the rest of the maze, these walls were smooth, like a pearl. The floors were carved with curly waves set in some sort of shiny black stone, and concave. At the center of the room, a tiny light, no bigger than a golf ball.

Mal swam and the little light became a Molly, standing in the center of the room, holding a stone.

It is hard to hug a person when you are wearing scuba gear, but Mal managed it, squeezing Molly so hard their helmets clanged together with a loud THWAK!

"Molly!" Mal cried.

Molly couldn't hear, but she could imagine Mal's voice, and she squeezed Mal back.

CHAPTER 41

By the time Mal and Molly and Deborah and Claudia made it back to the surface, a very anxious Ripley, April, and Jo were waiting.

"HIP HIP AMY RAY!" Ripley cheered, doing a Ripley dance of joy. "They're ALIVE!"

April ran to the water's edge as Mal's and Molly's heads finally appeared. "We were freaking out!"

"This is what it must feel like to be Jen," Jo observed, her hand on her chest.

"WHAT THE Desiree Akhavan, do NOT even joke about that." April shook her head. "I do not need that pressure."

"We should probably tell her where we are more often," Mal said, shaking the water out of her hair.

Ripley and Bubbles held out blankets for the scouts who had body temperatures. "You guys were in the water for so long. You're so PRUNEY!"

"Wait a nanosecond, Mal," April gasped. "YOU were in the WATER!"

Mal reached her hand out from under her blanket, grabbing Molly's frozen fingers. "Are you okay?"

"Look at you." Molly squeezed Mal's hand. "In a lake now like it's NBD!"

"I had to make sure you were safe," Mal said, pressing her forehead to Molly's.

"I was okay," Molly said with a small smile. "But I was still REALLY glad to see you."

"Did you get the Seal?" Heddie asked, still floating over the water.

"I did." Molly opened her blanket and held out her hand. "Or I think I did."

The object in Molly's hand looked like a stone record covered in a thick layer of brownish slime.

"You always want these old magic things to be just a little more majestic than they are." April sighed, running her finger through the slime, which peeled away like frosting on a cake. "Sometimes it's a sparkly stone and sometimes it's a little more unicorn fart."

"Ew," Jo said quietly.

Molly ran her hand over the stone, peeling back the last of the goo. "It's fine, it's just a little goopy."

Claudia hovered by the edge of the lake as Molly walked toward her, carrying the stone like a room service tray.

"So, here it is," Molly said, holding it out. "I don't know what you're supposed to do, but . . ."

"You need to make a wish." Deborah floated up next to Claudia. "It has to be a wish made by the living, the more the better. They all have to hold on to the stone and make a wish."

"Are you sure?" April asked.

"Yes." Deborah reached out to touch Claudia's braid. "I'm so sorry. I'm so sorry, Claudia."

Turning, Deborah held out her hands, like she was showing there was nothing in her left hand or right hand. "I'm sorry to all of you. This was all my fault."

"No, it wasn't." Claudia hovered, her outline flickering. "This was all *my* fault. I don't know what I was thinking."

Turning, Claudia took Deborah's hands in hers. "I'm not going."

"What?" April cried out. "But we DID THIS WHOLE THING TO G—"

Jo gave her a tiny push. "April."

"Sorry. Never mind." April grinned apologetically. "I meant, just . . . Yay!"

"No!" Deborah shook her head. "You wanted to leave! You should go!"

"Being a scout is about being there for your fellow scouts," Claudia sobbed. "Like Mal is for Molly and Molly is for Mal and Roanoke was for us."

"You are a great scout," Deborah insisted.

"But if I leave." Claudia dropped her head. "I won't be. If I leave, it will hurt you. And I just . . . I thought I could, but I can't do that."

Claudia let go of Deborah's hands. "So I'm staying."

CHAPTER 42

On the far side of the lake, standing in the marshes of reeds and cattails, Rosie was watching, a thermos of nettle tea in hand.

Taking a sip of piping hot tea, she sighed. "Hey, you old coot."

The faint sounds of bear paws in mud faded and became the smucks of a waddling Bearwoman. "Hey there, Red."

On the far edge of the lake, Rosie could see the soft glow of ghosts and hear the loud chirps of April echoing across the lake. "They found the Seal."

"You knew they would," Bearwoman snuffed, annoyed.

"I did." Rosie paused. "I'm glad they found Daedalus. It's good to have some phantom vibes in the camp."

"So you say." Bearwoman sniffed.

"They're our history," Rosie said.

Rosie was a huge fan of *The Pact*. She thought it was one of the better books written by a scout in the library.

"They stole a seal from a labyrinth," Bearwoman noted. "They're hardly model scouts."

"They wanted to stay scouts forever," Rosie said. "But yes, that's true. Still, I like having a little more ghost around."

"I always thought they should have called it Lake Mildred. Or Lochness Lake." Bearwoman shoved her hands in her pockets. "Whose brilliant idea was it to name the lake after the thing hiding at the bottom of it?"

"You'd have to dig into council records to find that out, or get some jam and ask Inez," Rosie said.

Bearwoman snorted.

"But I think the lake was named that because the Seal was meant to be found, as magical objects relating to wishes often are," Rosie said. "Plus, this gave Daedalus the possibility of undoing the wish if they so desired. The flip side of a pact made by scouts too young to understand its true meaning."

Bearwoman grumbled. "Big responsibility."

"They'll figure it out," Rosie said. "I trust them."

"Well, it's you that's putting it back when they're done." Bearwoman turned. "That water's freezing."

"I know it." Rosie took another sip from her thermos. "Sun's coming up."

"Bears don't care," Bearwoman retorted, and in a whirl of something very much like a handful of glitter being tossed into the air, a bear appeared and stalked off into the woods, muttering something about ghosts and vegetables.

CHAPTER 43

I t was Mal's idea to pack a picnic and go to her and Molly's special spot the next day.

To feel the sun on their shoulders and the warm breeze.

Jo and April and Ripley went off to kick some serious tail at foosball, and give Mal and Molly some space.

Pulling a jar of jam out of the picnic basket, Molly looked up at Mal. "Thanks for saving me."

"Like you said, you were kind of already saving yourself," Mal said, "with your cool yarn technique."

Molly smiled. "I guess, but I was really really glad when you showed up. My light was about to go. Not that I'm scared of the dark. But the bottom of a lake is DARK."

"I was really really glad to see you," Mal said. "Even though you were underwater in what was essentially a watery tomblike thing."

"It feels like maybe you're facing your fear of water," Molly said. "That's pretty cool."

"I'm not really so much afraid of water, I think." Mal looked down. "Sometimes I think I'm more scared of you."

"ME?" Molly's eyes went wide.

"Not YOU YOU." Mal grabbed Molly's hands. "I mean, just. When you're sad, I don't know why it scares me. But it does. I want to, like, rescue you from being sad. But I know that you can't actually do that."

"No, you can't," Molly agreed, finishing off her biscuit with Life's a Peach preserves made by BunBun.

"It's just . . . I know the stuff about your mom makes you sad," Mal said. "And I know thinking about going home makes you sad."

"Yeah, well." Molly looked up at the sky. "Yeah.

"I mean." Molly crossed her arms over her chest. "Yeah, I'm scared thinking about the fact that you're going to leave. That someday we'll ALL go home. And you're going to have this whole other world and I won't be in it. I'm scared thinking about what I'm going to be like when I'm not here."

"You know," Mal said, "no matter where I am, you will always be sitting here in my heart, so I'm NEVER EVER EVER going to forget about you."

Molly put her hands on her face and Mal wrapped her arms around Molly.

"I don't want to do stupid math homework," Molly sniffed.

"I'm going to bury that stupid math homework in a pile of unicorn droppings," Mal murmured into Molly's neck.

Which made Molly laugh. "That's very sweet. But please don't.

"You know," Molly said, wiping her tears with her sleeve, "even though I'm afraid of going home, I still know that Claudia deserves to leave. I can see that, right?"

"Right," Mal said. "But it will probably make you sad if she leaves."

"Yeah," Molly said, lying down on her back. "But that's okay."

Mal laid down on the blanket next to Molly. Up above, the clouds all looked like hearts. Sort of. Mal willed them to be heart clouds sailing over their heads.

"They sort of look like hearts," Molly said, pointing.

"Agreed," Mal said, taking Molly's hand.

It was a perfect summer day. One of many days that both Mal and Molly would hold in their hearts for all time.

CHAPTER 44

Claudia was sitting alone on the bridge when Mal found her that night, her arms wrapped around her knees.

In the moonlight, Claudia's shape was a silver shadow. Her hair glowed as she twisted her braid around her finger, looking at the sky, full of stars instead of clouds.

"Do you ever miss the sun?" Mal asked, stepping onto the bridge.

"No," Claudia sighed. "I always liked the moon and stars. It's something Deborah and I always had in common."

Mal put a foot on the bridge. "Have you changed your mind?"

"About leaving?" Claudia floated in front of Mal. "No."

"I think you should go," Mal said. "I think you should let us make this wish for you."

"No." Claudia shook her head. "I will not be the cause of sadness."

"You know," Mal said, running her fingers through her hair, "Daedalus loves you and they want this for you. They want you to go see the world outside Miss Qiunzella's, you know? And believe me, like, I've only seen a little bit and it's pretty cool."

"I am sure, but . . ." Claudia squeezed her knees tight, like she was holding herself together. "I cannot stop thinking about the pain it will cause them, on top of the pain they've already suffered . . . for me. Maybe I refused to think about it before. Then I saw you and Molly. I saw the look on Deborah's face when we were by the labyrinth. Now . . ."

"You know," Mal said, "it's okay for them to be sad. They'll miss you and you'll miss them. Sometimes sad is just a memory in your heart. Daedalus knows you'll be doing something that makes you happy and that will make them happy."

"It will," Maggie said, appearing on the bridge. "You stupid carrot."

"Do not call her stupid." Deborah frowned, appearing next to Maggie. "Claudia is not stupid."

"You may not be the smartest Lumberghost," Heddie said, appearing next to Claudia, "but I'm going to miss you lots all the same."

Claudia's form shivered in the moonlight. "No," she said.

"Yes," Deborah said, floating closer. "Yes, Claudia. We all agree."

"Hey," Maggie added, "at least you got us some new friends. That is a pretty good scout turn."

"And no matter what," Deborah said, pulling Claudia into a big ghost hug, "you will always be a Lumberjane, a part of Daedalus in life and death."

"Oh," Claudia wailed, "I did not know it would be like this!"

Standing next to the lake, Mal, Molly, Ripley, Jo, and Bubbles watched as Daedalus all said the rest of their goodbyes, things too ghostly for human ears, things a scout has to say after a life and afterlife of knowing another scout.

A million little goodbyes whispered under the light of the moon over Lake Specter.

CHAPTER 45

Every day, people make wishes.

Some are small, like "I wish I could find my slippers."

Some are much bigger. Some are impossible. Some only seem that way.

There are some wishes made more powerful by the people present.

Some wishes are made possible by magical things like the Specter's Seal, a Seal that had been wished upon six times, twice by Lumberjanes.

The scouts of Daedalus made their wish a century ago.

Now, while the scouts of Roanoke cabin stood on the island at the center of Lake Specter, holding the Seal, Daedalus watched from the bridge.

As Claudia floated up into the sky over Roanoke, Deborah thought about the night they found the Seal. She thought about the cookies they'd stowed in their skirt pockets. About the bug bites they all had on their ankles and the grass that was in her hair from slipping down the hill when Maggie lost her footing and pulled her down with her. She thought about the first time she laid eyes on the Seal, an object that would change her life for more than forever.

And now, impossibly, it was about to give Claudia a second chance at the afterlife.

"I hope you have fun, Claudia!" Ripley chirped, stepping up to the Seal.

"Have great adventures," April said, lifting the Seal with both hands.

"Learn new amazing things," Jo said, taking her side of the Seal.

"Have fun in New York," Molly said, sliding her hand under the Seal. "And everywhere else you go."

"We'll miss you," Mal said, gripping the Seal tightly.

Claudia hovered above them, over the Specter's Seal, now gripped in all of Roanoke's able hands.

"Make a wish," Deborah whispered.

Heddie and Maggie held each other.

Molly nodded. "Ready?"

"Ready," the rest of Roanoke said.

"Yes," Claudia said. "Goodbye."

Gripping the Seal, in their minds Roanoke saw a picture of Claudia floating through the world, seeing all the things she wanted to see, outside the gates of Miss Qiunzella's.

"Goodbye, dear friend," Deborah said.

A flash of light exploded out of the Seal, a bright green light that swallowed the island and everyone, dead and alive, on it.

April would try to describe it later as not emerald or mint, but like if emerald and mint had a party and filled it with a giant spark of energy and then blew that up.

The light was there and then, as quickly as it came, it was gone.

And so was Claudia.

CHAPTER 46

The next day, when Molly woke up, she knew it was going to be a really amazing day at camp.

The sun was out and there wasn't a cloud in the sky.

Ripley started the day leading a Jazzercise class with Barney, whose high kicks were getting better and better every week.

Jo started the day in the shop finishing up the work she'd started with Heddie, adjusting some wiring on their soon-to-be-completed boxcar, Laverne. Which was lighter than Heddie ever could have imagined possible and very very fast.

April spent the day writing so seriously and intently that she eventually drew the interest of Rosie, who was passing by with a bag of what looked like blue ping-pong balls, but alive?

Maybe.

"What are you up to, scout?" Rosie asked.

"It's a new genre," April said, looking up from her notepad. "Creative Fantasy Non-Fiction."

"Interesting," Rosie said.

"Maybe not a new new genre," April admitted. "It's somewhat inspired by some alumnae creative works that I've been reading lately."

"Some very inspiring writers have come through these lands," Rosie agreed.

April bent her head back down.

"What are you going to call it?" Rosie asked.

"Right now it's just called *The Lumberjanes*," April admitted. "But I'm open to new titles."

"Keep it simple." Rosie gave a thumbs-up. "Oh, and thank you for the Seal."

"No problem." April nodded. "Let us know if you want to borrow some equipment to put it back."

"I'll manage, thank you, scout," Rosie said.

And then, as was Rosie's way, she walked off to do whatever it is Rosie does.

April licked her lips and tapped her pencil on her pad. There were so many adventures a person could potentially write about. It was impossible to choose.

"I'll just have to write about all of them," she told herself.

Better get started.

Meanwhile, over at a picnic bench, Mal and Molly spent the day working on their accordion duet, having recently switched to "Closer to Fine."

Looking over her accordion, Mal grinned. "Is it me or is today an amazing day to be a Lumberjane?"

"I was just thinking that." Molly smiled.

Because, okay, it's been said, but it's true, every day really is a great day to be a Lumberjane.

Especially when you get to share it with someone awesome.

SOME LUMBERJANES BADGES!

BERRY DELICIOUS

Pie? Oh MY! Scouts with this badge will master the art of combining fruit and sugar to make edible masterpieces with and without pastry.

AN HERB IN THE HAND

Want some sage advice? Scouts with this badge know the difference between basils and make the best omelettes and salads. Get ahead of the herb with this comprehensive guide to plants that make things taste better.

WATER SAFETY RULES!

No running in the pool. No diving in shallow water. Stay safe in and out of the water with this handy badge of safety know-how.

SNAP!

Take a picture, it will last longer! Black-and-white, color, and instant-film masterpieces are possible with this badge for avid shutterbugs.

MAKI ME A BELIEVER

On a roll? Take the next step in your culinary journey with this badge, covering everything you need to complete this prized Japanese food.

EVERYTHING'S PARANORMAL

Why be normal when you can be paranormal? Explore the unexplained with this badge that asks scouts to dig into those phenomena that defy traditional explanation.

SHAVE THE WAY

Hairstyling is all the BUZZ with this badge for future haircutters and fans of the close cut.

SOCK IT TO ME

Like to knit, purl, and keep your feet— and the feet of your friends—warm and cozy? Then this badge is for you! Pick up your needles, your hooks, and your yarn and knit your socks ON!

ONE WHEEL OR ANOTHER

Life is all about balance, especially when you only have one wheel. This badge may take a few tries to master, but once you do, uni won't regret it.

BOOK AND SEE LIBRARY PIN

The library offers scouts a world of knowledge. Take advantage of all the resources it offers with this badge especially for bookworms.

MAKE IT TORQUE

May the rotational force be with you! Keep up your momentum with this badge that gives scouts more insight into how to make things go.

IT'S POPPIN'

Want to make your dance moves POP on the dance floor? Learn the basics of popping and locking and show us your moves!

HOP, SKIP, AND A JUMP

Some of the best badges need the least equipment. All you need for this badge is a rope and some rhythm. Don't get all tied up! Keep your feet moving!

JETÉ, SET, GO!

Might as well jump! With this badge you can learn how to leave the ground with style and grace, with an equally balletic landing.

BECAUSE I HAVE A HAMMER

If you have a hammer, some nails, and a little arm power, you can make just about anything with this badge that teaches scouts some basics of carpentry magic.

I SPIDER

I Spider, with my little eye, something that has eight legs, spins webs, and scares the living daylights out of some people. Scouts with this badge learn more about these very curious arthropods, these amazing arachnids that have inspired so many stories.

TAKE IT OR LAKE IT

Dive deep into the world of lakes and discover the secrets of the deep blue with this badge for water lovers.

MARIKO TAMAKI

is a writer known for her graphic novel
This One Summer, a Caldecott Honor and
Printz Honor winner, cocreated with
her cousin Jillian Tamaki, among other
notable novels. See her work at
marikotamaki.blogspot.com.

BROOKLYN ALLEN

is a cocreator and the original illustrator
of the Lumberjanes graphic novel series
and a graduate of the Savannah College
of Art and Design. Brooklyn's website is
brooklynaallen.tumblr.com.

COLLECT THEM ALL!

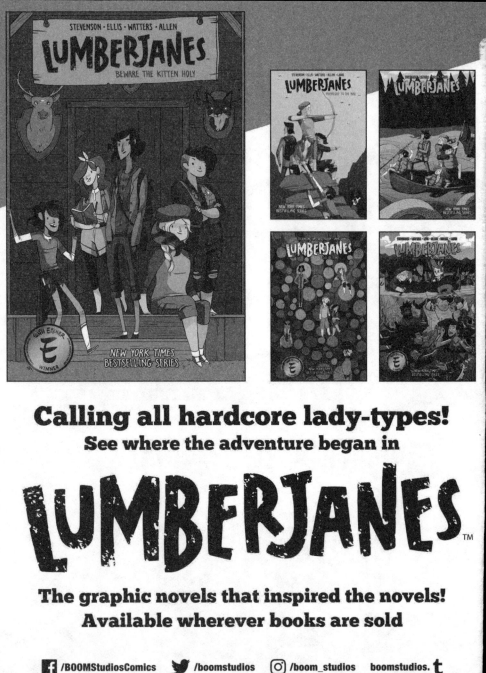